THE

BURROWING RODENT

EMPIRE

ORIGINS

BY

DILLON WILLETT

ILLUSTRATIONS BY ALEXANDRE AUGUSTO

This is a work of fiction, and the views expressed herein are the sole responsibility of the author. Likewise, certain characters, places, and incidents are the product of the author's imagination, and any resemblance to actual person, living or dead, or actual events or places, is entirely coincidental.

The Burrowing Rodent Empire: Origins

ISBN (Paperback): 979-8-9952276-1-8

ISBN (Hardcover): 979-8-9952276-2-5

This book is dedicated to my family and the handlers out there who've backed Gopherit from the start.

Gopherit grew into more than a brand. It became a shared world. A lot of the details in these pages were sparked by the jokes, comments, ideas, and art you all put into it. That feedback loop was the push I needed to start writing, keep going, and actually finish.

Thank you for the support and the love.

If you want to dive deeper, join an art competition, or find the short-form field reports, start here: **gopheritshop.com**

"What will you, gopher next?"

TABLE OF CONTENTS

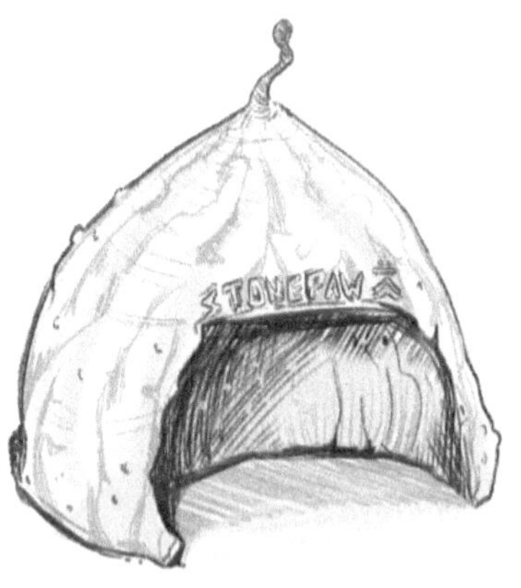

CHAPTER 1 | EYES

Thick dust sealed Mari's eyelashes shut as cool, dank air enveloped her still form. She drew a ragged breath that caught, the dust heavy in her lungs. One arm swept out to trace the dirt-laden stone floor while the other paw rubbed her eyes free. A faint blue glow pooled in the cavern's corner, delicate and steady. She blinked into it, and her pupils widened.

She sat up. A shattered mural stretched across the wall in front of her, fractured and scarred into illegibility. Overhead, stalactites hung, their tips lost in shadow. Sulfur stung her nostrils as she inhaled.

Mari searched her mind for how she'd ended up here, but the memories eluded her, fragments of a dream slipping away.

I'll figure out what's going on, even if I can't remember how I got here.

Struggling to stand, she raised her arms overhead in a deep stretch. *How long have I been lying like that?* A shiver of uncertainty ran up her spine. Her stomach growled. She put a paw to it, as if pressure alone could calm the gnawing.

Must have been ages. I haven't been this hungry since the war.

A scan of the chamber drew her toward the sole source of light. Recognition lifted her face. Her lantern. Picking it up, she turned the compact rectangular prism over in her paws, inspecting it for damage. She wiped the opaque emitters clean, then clipped it back onto the shoulder strap of her pack.

Under the cool, milky-blue glow, the surrounding space sharpened.

Back at the chamber's center, Mari noticed the walls formed a rough arch filled with rubble, like a passage collapsed on purpose. Or crushed by time. She crouched where she had awoken and ran a nail along the ground. The dust held a shallow impression of her body.

Was I carried here? There would be tracks. Someone else's. Something. Anything.

None. No tracks led to this spot, Mari's or otherwise.

The mural drew her closer. In the lantern's light, the details gained depth, shadows catching in every crack and gouge. The mural stretched the full length of the wall. Much of it had deep scratches that broke it into pieces and defaced it, leaving large sections illegible.

In the center sat an emblem marked with three diamonds. They formed a triangle. The bottom two joined at their middle points, with the third set above to complete the shape. A ring enclosed the diamonds. Beneath it, sharp lines joined in grouped segments of varying length, like a language made of angles.

Mari dropped her pack off one shoulder and swung it around in front of her. Rifling through it, she pulled out a metal cylinder and a small piece of chalk. Unscrewing the end exposed a roll of parchment. She drew it out and flattened it over the emblem.

Holding the chalk flat against the parchment, she rubbed quickly, transferring the outline of the symbol and its markings in pale, dusty strokes.

I'll bring this back to The Burrow. Rufus might know something.

She tucked the parchment away and closed the cylinder, then crossed the chamber to the blocked passage. A crisp breeze pressed through the cracks between the boulders. Both paws found the debris as she leaned in, then turned her head and rested an ear against the loose wall.

Only her heartbeat answered, loud in the silence.

A few steps back gave her space to think. *Okay. A mind blast could clear this.* The thought tightened her chest. In class, it usually came up empty. Still, Mister Craghorb's lesson.

Clear your mind and… She paused, breath held. *I almost forgot.*

She knelt by her pack and pulled out what looked like a petrified watermelon half. Precisely engraved across the brow read Stonepaw, preceded by a series of nested chevrons topped with a bar and two dots. She spun it around, lifted it over her tiny head, and set the helmet firmly in place. The world narrowed as it gathered her mind, shielding the noise from her thought.

With the pack on her back again, Mari refocused on the rubble pile. Paws came tight to her chest, shoulders rounding forward, fingers curved around an empty sphere. The same mental pep talk restarted, one she'd used a hundred times in class.

Okay, clear your mind, clear your mind and focus on the intent.

Her palms rotated outward toward the loose stone as her chest opened and her gaze fixed on the wall. She felt something internal catch, like a hook in her mind. *Let the intent move through you and see it thro—*

A blast reverberated through the space. Mari's lantern shuddered, and dust choked the air. Her short, smooth fur stood on end as static snapped between the fibers. A moment later, the sounds of rock and rubble impacting somewhere beyond the chamber echoed back around her.

Her throat seized. A hard cough punched out into the dark. The effort left a metallic taste in her mouth as pressure welled like she'd clenched a muscle deep inside her skull.

It worked. It actually worked.

Warm sunlight broke through the swirling dust, reflecting off millions of suspended particles. The glinting haze coalesced into familiar shapes. Almond eyes guided her vision to a thick nose resting above a mouth interrupted by two smooth teeth. Coarse hair framed the features. The space held like a breath, then let go, and fragrant air rushed inward through the new opening.

Mom?

Her unease faded, replaced by warmth. Nostalgia washed over her and brought her back to the days before the war, when she was small and her mother's unrelenting affection dominated her world.

She scrambled over the pile of debris, chunks of rock shifting underfoot. *Nuts. Wish that one had been in class. Maybe then the others would stop acting like I can't manifest at all.*

As Mari moved into the next room, she found the source of the daylight. An opening nearly forty tails up cut a pale rectangle into the stone. *No second chances from that high.* A rope hung from the edge all the way to the floor, its slack coiled at the base. She looked back at the passage she had just come through.

Most of the chamber was lined with unremarkable rock walls, but the doorway itself was different. Sculpted images of burrowing rodents framed it ornately. Some battled fish. Others defended against aerial assaults from birds. Near the top was a bipedal creature that Mari had never seen before. Surrounded by burrowing rodents of all types, it looked less like a threat and more like a partner. A friend.

She reached out a paw. As it drew near the carvings, a wave of energy pulsed through the inscriptions. Reflexively, she withdrew. She paused, then reached back to see if it would happen again.

Nothing.

Mari studied the scene a while longer, committing what she could to memory, then made her way to the rope. She climbed toward the opening, broke into the light, and ascended into the day.

Her eyes squinted. The setting sun was intense.

She pulled off the helmet and slid it into her pack, then reached into her vest pocket and pulled out a pair of shades. Donning them instantly relieved her eyes. The round frames mechanically expanded a thin layer of canvas that covered even the sides, effectively sealing her from the light.

Mari surveyed her surroundings. She knew she was at the north end of Long Valley. Scrub and stubby pine trees marked the red rocky landscape. Nearby mountains towered, lining the horizon in all directions. Beside the opening she had just climbed from, sat a large boulder. Fresh drag tracks betrayed any secret that it had once covered this entrance.

No way I moved that, unless… I manifested like that before. Before I woke up here.

She drew a breath, pressed her tongue to her big flat incisors, and released it into a powerful whistle.

From a nearby bush, a large rabbit leapt out, dark tan fur peppered with black and white markings. Its sail-like ears eclipsed the sun. Mari guessed it was just over an hour from slipping below the horizon.

Relief softened her face into a smile. "Ah, there you are, my beautiful boy," she said, patting his muscular haunch.

His nose twitched vigorously, each nostril flaring and shifting as it searched for rogue scents. Glossy eyes, empty of thought, stared toward the horizon.

A riding harness, saddle, and bags were strapped to him. Mari reached into one of the saddlebags and pulled out another long tube. She unscrewed the flat cap and withdrew a thick roll of well-used paper.

"Alright, Phlip," she said, glancing between him and the landscape. "What were we doing out here? And why can't I remember anything?"

She unfurled a large map, turning Phlip's backside into an impromptu table. Her thin finger traced the route back home.

"I'm not seeing any notes…" She gave him a side-eye. "You remember anything?"

Phlip dropped a few quick pellets onto the dry, rocky ground.

"Yeah. Thought not," Mari muttered. "Alright. Let's get home before dark. The birds will be out soon."

She grabbed Phlip's harness and, in one swift motion, levered herself into the saddle, then kicked firmly with her heels. Off they went, bounding down the valley at high speed.

As they wove through familiar terrain, the last bits of bright blue of daylight faded and were replaced by deep warm hues. The clouds shifted into light pink puffs, stretched by the wind. Mari turned the strange events over in her mind, trying to remember what she had been doing before waking in that chamber. The last thing that surfaced was a conversation with her friend Jerro. He was an engineer from Deepworks, a subsurface dam and power station. But it had been ordinary. They'd been talking about her upcoming psionics exams and what she planned to do after the academy.

The wind whipped through her fur. "Well," she said to Phlip but mostly to herself. "I suppose that's somewhere to start."

Ahead, ancient megalithic ruins lined a wide path of crumbled black gravel that stretched down the rocky trough and into a narrow pass leading out of Long Valley. A distant cawing snapped her back to the danger of being exposed on the surface. Instinctively, she pulled her body tight to Phlip, pressing her chest into his back. She tilted her head toward the sound and spotted two winged forms approaching.

Ruins are bad luck. Birds. Birds are worse.

A bent metal stick held the twisted remains of a red octagonal panel. The turnoff point. Mari pulled Phlip's reins hard and directed him sharply into the ruins. She slid her leg over and dismounted in one motion. Together they ducked under a rectangular gray pillar that had toppled and come to rest on another dilapidated structure. Rusted sticks of ribbed metal protruded from its broken end, tangled in each other's grasp.

Mari and Phlip slipped into a windowless room and hunkered down in a nook. Dust coated everything. Framed compartments rose to the high ceiling, their contents long since scavenged. Shards of glass littered the black-and-white checkered floor. Some sections were torn away to reveal a yellowed underlayer. A smooth red counter was tilted against the main entrance. It struggled to prop up part of the collapsing roof, bracing against time and gravity.

Two sets of sweeping wings disturbed the silence. The clacking of talons replaced them on the firm surface outside. Mari looked into Phlip's eye, placed a paw on his ear, and pressed a finger to her pursed lips.

The tapping shifted to a sharp crunch as something entered the decaying building.

A loud squawk startled Mari, and she drew closer to Phlip. She could feel his heart pounding fast and hard, but his face stayed ignorantly stoic, as if he still hadn't decided this was dangerous. More cawing followed, an exchange between the two birds. The sheen of deep black plumage flashed in the shelving gaps. Mari was frozen in fear. Then there was a loud scuff, and the clatter of claws retreated.

Mari let out a slow breath as the sounds disappeared entirely.

After another moment of silence, they returned to their path. Twilight had taken over, and stars began to poke through the darkening violet sky. The landscape softened as they rode, shifting into verdant foliage. Clusters of towering trees gathered along a creek, tracing its path like a dark ribbon.

Mari guided Phlip toward the thick, meandering line of vegetation and used it as cover. They had transitioned into the foothills now, and the hidden entrance to The Burrow wasn't much farther.

A downed tree signaled the location.

She rode up and hopped off Phlip's back, then quickly scanned the area. Her paw found a familiar limb worn smooth from use. She gave it a twist. A mechanical click answered, and a small metal pad slid into view as the tree shifted.

Without waiting for it to fully open, Mari pressed her paw onto it. A red light glowed beneath her skin, then flipped to green and faded out.

The gray mass of wood hinged at one end. Soft lights, similar to Mari's lantern, lined a descending ramp and spilled outward into the night like a quiet invitation. Mari led the way with Phlip close at heel, and they began to descend.

The chirping of crickets faded behind them. A deep thud followed.

Mari glanced back as the entrance resealed.

CHAPTER 2 | THE BURROW

As Mari walked down the path into The Burrow, the familiar muffled sounds of hustle and bustle gradually grew. She had used this entrance many times throughout her life. It was a shared secret among academy aspirants. With Phlip hopping along at her side, she approached a circular slab of stone that terminated the hall.

At the center of the stone was a small hexagonal depression. Mari pulled a silver pendant from beneath her vest, pressed it into the concavity where it fit with satisfying precision, and focused her mind on the door. It jarred and shifted forward, rough-cut edges revealing themselves as it moved. Loose dust fell as the slab rolled to the side and disappeared into a pocket formed by the adjoining wall. Aromatic scents washed over Mari's nose, reminding her stomach that it still had an unresolved issue, while crowd chatter pressed in around her.

The door opened into one of the darker alleys. Mari stepped out carefully with Phlip trailing close. Behind them, the large stone door rolled back into place. On this side, it was marked with a worn yellow number twelve, blending in as just another maintenance passage for sewer and utility access.

Mari moved quickly out of the empty alley and wove into the bustling street. Above, vaulted ceilings were dimly lit by the warm glow of bioluminescent roots and fungi. The smell of perfectly roasted butter-stick potatoes hit her like a tunnel collapse, and her stomach growled in response. She turned toward the vendor and placed her paws on the edge of the cart, pulling her face up to peer over it.

A large marmot in a grease-splattered apron stood behind the cart. Steam rose from the skewers along the cart's edge.

"That'll be two greens!" he beamed.

Mari shot a paw into her vest pocket. Three triangular stones greeted her. She looked up at the marmot, turned her paw over, and presented the blue gems. "I've only got three blues. Would you do a half potato?"

The marmot leaned forward and looked her over, taking in the little gopher swimming in the oversized vest and the academy pendant resting on her chest. A grin spread across his face, and he winked. "Well, why didn't you mention you're an aspirant? How about I give you the discount? One potato for…" He paused, glanced at her paw, then back to her. "Three blues!"

He popped a skewered potato free and extended it down. Mari reached up and slid the gems onto the corner of the cart. A shy smile tugged across her face as she thanked him.

Phlip nosed her shoulder. Mari turned to see his large glassy eye nearly touching hers. His gaze dropped to the potato.

Mari hesitated, then broke it in half. She popped one piece into Phlip's mouth as he fidgeted with excitement.

She ate while the crowd swept them through Merchant Hollow, one of The Burrow's busiest digs. Shops climbed the walls and curled into the ceiling, held by twisted roots and stacked stone. Almost anything could be found here. Food, psionic amplifiers, elixirs, codices, even pre-war tech if you knew which offshoot to follow.

The crowd chatter was typical, but something caught Mari's attention. A knot of rodents had gathered close, looking over their shoulders and tightening their circle. Mari slowed just enough to pass within earshot.

A young black-and-white hamster whispered, "My cousin, the one in Shadowpaw, said there was suspicious activity in Deepworks earlier."

"That's a load of worms," a tan shrew snapped. "The Builders would *never* let anything happen to Deepworks. It's too important to The Burrow. Plus, that new guy runs a tight burrow. What's his name again?"

A mottled chocolate-and-cream gerbil cut in. "Ordinate Rull."

"Yeah. Good beaver. Everything'll be fine. After all, packed earth outlasts panic." The shrew delivered it like a verdict.

Mari fell back into the flow and glanced at Phlip. "Jerro might be off shift. Tailweaver's on the way. Wanna check?" Phlip hopped along, unbothered.

Mari pulled the last of the potato off the skewer with her teeth. "Yeah. Jerro'll know."

They rounded a corner into a narrow alley that ended abruptly at towering wooden double doors. Arched stained-glass windows flanked the entry. Above it, Tailweaver's curved in bold black letters, the inlaid glass catching the glow and casting amber ripples onto the stone.

Mari pulled the brass latch. The door gave, and light poured into the alley. Tea and dusty old books wrapped around her, replacing Merchant Hollow's earth-and-spice as she slipped inside with Phlip close behind.

A stout, bespectacled hedgehog sat cross-legged in a plush maroon corner chair, puffing on a pipe. Vanilla smoke rose from it, drifting up through the warmth of a central stone hearth. Not one fireplace, but a split rectangle, half hanging from the ceiling and half set into the floor. Flames danced between the sections. It crackled softly. Bookshelves climbed to the ceiling, with a track ladder clipped along the top row. Mismatched furniture filled the room, gathered over years. Every piece, a quiet invitation to stay, and a story of its own to share. In the opposite corner, a round-eared gray chinchilla and a tri-colored guinea pig in glasses bent over a heavy text, murmuring as they read.

Mari crossed to the back hall. A short bookshelf stood beneath a gold filigree-framed illustration of a ship in a terrible storm, waves breaking over the deck.

Two worn wooden doors faced each other. Behind her, Phlip settled against the warm stone.

A sign on the left door showed a pile of small oval pellets, and the door hung ajar, revealing a toilet and washbasin. The opposite door was shut, a stained placard above it engraved: Rufus.

Mari leaned in, listened, then knocked.

"Not in this lune," the hedgehog called.

Mari poked her head back into the main room. "Oh, thanks Xan. Do you know where he is?"

"No idea. He was here earlier, then popped off without a word."

Mari turned to the chinchilla and guinea pig. "How about Jerro? You seen him around?"

The guinea pig shook her head, then glanced at the chinchilla. "Not today. Not since we got here."

Mari let out a small puff of air. "Alright, thanks." Her eyes caught on their oversized book as she drifted closer. "What're you reading?"

The guinea pig tipped the cover up without losing her place. "The Prime History of The Burrow, by Yari Highpaw."

"Underrated historian," Xan added from across the room, the pipe still clenched between his teeth. "Great writer too."

"Actually…" The chinchilla pushed the book open and flipped toward the back, the pages thumping down on the guinea pig's book-mark arm. "There's a section on the Great Bird War. Outriders, founding, all of it. And there's a picture." He rifled faster, then froze. "Isn't this your mom?"

Mari stepped in beside them. A gentle smile found her face. "Yeah," she said softly. "That's her."

She traced the monochrome line. Gophers sat mounted on long-eared, peppered rabbits, striped helmets capped on their heads. Her finger stopped on a small gopher with gracile features, reins gripped tight, gaze pulled off-scene with the others.

"Dad too." Mari pointed to the rider beside her mother. He sat proud, a head taller than her mom.

"I can't believe I've never seen this picture," Mari said. "Dad never talks about it." The smile slipped.

The guinea pig leaned around her. "Hey Alfie. Can I have my arm back now?"

Alfie blinked and flipped the pages back. "Sorry, Jess."

Jess tugged her arm free and shook it out. "No worries. But a fresh cup of tea wouldn't hurt," she said, then took a swig from her chipped mug and held it out toward Alfie.

Mari crossed back to Phlip and ran a paw down his back. "Thanks for showing me that," she said, looking over her shoulder. "I'll read it later. Come on, Phlip. Let's head home."

They rejoined the crowd in Merchant Hollow. The tunnel widened, and a cooler, deep magenta glow filled the passage as the crowd thinned. She was nearing The Spine, the central column of The Burrow, spiraling upward to connect the sub-corridors. It rose through a small opening to the surface. Through it, a thin slice of night sky showed. Moonlight slipped down through the gap, the only sky many there would ever see.

Ascending through The Spine's center was an imposing crystalline structure, the source of the light. A pair of robed rats knelt beside it, eyes closed. A river of light meandered to their foreheads and settled between their brows. As the moonlight strengthened overhead, the crystal shifted toward deep blue. Nearby shop signs followed suit, their hues turning with the crystal's pulse.

"New lune," one of the rats murmured. The other echoed it like a habit.

"Miss Stonepaw," a shrill voice called out behind her.

Mari stopped and turned slowly.

Mister Craghorb stood in the middle of the street, a small ground squirrel with long, wispy eyebrows and a maroon robe. He pierced her with squinted eyes.

"Miss Stonepaw…" His voice was strangely deep yet squeaky as he approached, inspecting her more closely, his gaze dropping to her feet before snapping back to her eyes. "We missed you at lessons today. I assumed perhaps you were unwell… but your constitution seems to be in good quality."

Mari glanced at Phlip without moving her head, then back to Mister Craghorb. "Mister Craghorb, my father's sick. I've been caring for him all day. You know it's just the two of us." She added quickly, "I ran out to get quantum blue carrot matrices. They help."

"Alright, young lady," he squeaked, turning away dismissively. Then he stopped and turned back. "I don't have to remind you, it's been eight cycles since a gopher has been admitted to the Yarrow Academy for Gifted Rodents?"

"I do, Mister Craghorb." Mari steadied her voice. "And I'm sorry I missed class. I'll make up the work. Promise."

He stepped closer, keeping his voice low. "Mari, I know you and your father don't have the same luxuries as many of the other aspirants. Tutors. Private lessons. That sort of thing." He studied her before continuing. "And I may not be your favorite instructor, but I push most where I see the greatest potential."

Without another word, he patted Mari's shoulder and resumed taking his leave. As he shuffled away, he shot a final glance over his shoulder, the corner of a grin showing.

Mari waved awkwardly and hurried off with Phlip toward the pathway that wound up the perimeter wall of The Spine. She turned down the dig that led to her den.

"Why'd he look at my feet?" she asked Phlip as she glanced down.

Rusty dirt caked her paws. The kind only found high up Long Valley.

∞

Her den had a large courtyard, especially for this dig. The ceiling roots gave off a calm, familiar glow, the kind that never flickered and never fully left a corner dark. In one corner sat a mat of straw. Mari led Phlip in, and he joyously hopped over to the worn bedding.

She pulled fresh hay from a storage bin near the porch and filled a bowl with water from a spigot.

"Sleep well, pal," she whispered as he munched away.

Mari moved to the circular stone door that served as the entrance to her den. She placed her paw on the groove running around its edge and gently rolled it to the right into a pocket in the earthen wall. While it was only halfway open, she slipped inside and quietly closed it behind her.

Sweetness hit the moment she stepped in. She rushed into the kitchen. A pot of caramelized carrot soup cooled on the counter beside an empty bowl and wooden spoon. Mari filled the bowl and shoveled it down, warm and creamy, with a sugary roasted bite.

The den was silent, except for a muffled voice seeping from her father's bedroom. She recognized the cadence immediately. As she neared the open passage, the sound swelled to full volume.

A gregarious voice boomed through the room. "Greetings, contestants and listeners! I'm your host Bobber Broadtail, and this is How Deep Can We Dig! Brought to you by Beaverwave Broadcasting! Today, we are putting up two of our returning contestants, Cluver and Cloe, the dynamic duo hailing from Merchant Hollow, to see if they can solve the mystery that our riddle masters have spun!"

Mari paused at the passage and watched her father's chest rise and fall with each snore. The far wall of his room was plastered with pictures of the two of them. Her first day of Burrow School. The day he taught her to ride Phlip. A picture of her holding her acceptance letter to the academy. Centered on the wall was a painted portrait of her mother, her father, and her as a pup.

He choked and rolled slightly, struggling to breathe.

Mari took a step into the room, opened his door further, then stopped herself. His breathing returned to a normal cadence.

"Sleep well, Dad," she whispered, and quietly went to her own room.

She flopped onto her bed and stared into the darkness. Her bedroom sat back from the courtyard, tucked into the earth where the walls kept the air cool and still. The bed felt like a pocket of safety, a low wooden frame with a thick mattress and layered quilts that held her in place, the way it always had. Her pillow carried a faint, clean scent of dried grass.

Her eyes wandered to the desk against the far wall. She could just make out the cluttered stacks of paper, charcoal sticks, and sketches pinned and layered over one another. Some were familiar, quick studies of Long Valley. Slopes and grasses, a line of trees, the suggestion of a trail she'd walked before. Others came from some-where else entirely, places her paws had never touched. Vistas too wide, skies that felt wrong in the best way, and shapes she couldn't name but kept drawing anyway, as if her mind knew them before she did.

A soft aquamarine light pulsed to life from a small stone set into the wall beside her headboard, projecting slow abstract shapes across the ceiling. The patterns stretched, softened, and dissolved, like ripples seen from below the surface.

∞

Mari was floating.

Weightless. Suspended in something warm and dense, like liq-uid, though she wasn't struggling to breathe. Calm seeped through her thoughts, dulling the edges of awareness. She raised a paw to her face and touched something smooth and unfamiliar.

A mask.

It covered her mouth and nose. Ribbed tubes extended from its sides, pulsing faintly. Panic flickered, brief and distant, before the calm pressed it back down.

Through blurred vision, she lifted her paw again, but it wasn't a paw.

Hairless. Pale. Long fingers extended from a wide, flat palm. It moved when she told it to, yet it felt wrong. Not hers.

A sudden surge of force tore through the stillness.

The warmth vanished. Gravity returned all at once. Mari was expelled, dropped or thrown, from whatever had held her. She struck cold stone and gasped as the shock rattled through her body.

She lay shivering, breath coming in broken pulls, the darkness around her thick and shifting. Shadows flowed like smoke along the walls, folding over themselves.

Then the stone beside her began to glow.

Lines traced themselves into existence, warming the darkness with soft amber light. Symbols and letters emerged, familiar, impossibly so. The same language she had seen carved into the cave walls.

Images followed.

Celestial bodies drifted across the surface. Long, thin creatures moved in silence. Unfamiliar rodents stood beneath vast skies. Sleek parabolic ships cut through space in tight formation.

Last, the symbol appeared.

Nested diamonds, circumscribed and precise. It burned brighter than the rest. Beneath it, an inscription began to form.

Before she could focus, before the meaning could settle—

∞

"Mari!"

She jolted awake.

Her father stood over her, his face tight with urgency. "Mari. We've got to evacuate. There's been an incident at Deepworks. The Burrow's flooding." He grabbed her paw. "Quickly. There isn't much time."

Mari sprang up, snagging her pack as her father pulled her toward the door. Once outside, she overtook him as he slowed and doubled over coughing. She whistled sharply.

Phlip leapt over the fence and joined her in stride.

The main corridor was filled with rushing water up to their waists. Other residents poured from their dens and sloshed through the main thoroughfare toward The Spine. Upstream, a large family of prairie dogs attempted to ford the torrent. Two pups were swept up, crying out for help.

Mari swung onto Phlip's back and outstretched an arm toward her dad. His paw gripped halfway up her forearm, and she hauled him onto the rabbit's strong back. Phlip's powerful build held steady in the rapids as they dodged debris and moved along the edges of the flood, leaping across courtyards.

As they made swift progress, Mari pointed back to two tan dots swirling down the dig toward them. "Dad, those are the Graslow pups!"

"Get us to that fence line," he said, pointing to the arched entrance of a connecting dig where a courtyard fence abutted.

Mari guided Phlip to the spot and they dismounted quickly. Her dad grabbed a rope from Phlip's saddle and started wrapping it around his midsection.

Mari snatched the other end and tied it around herself. "Dad, I'm going out there, not you. You and Phlip reel me back in."

He looked at her, bewildered. "I'm not letting you go out there."

"Dad, you won't make it. This isn't a debate."

She finished the knot, dropped her pack, and before he could stop her, she vaulted the fence and plunged into the freezing, turbid water. Fighting the current, she swam out, planning her intercept course for the pups.

They had split. Mari set her sights on the farther one and drove forward, paw over paw, fighting the pull of the river.

A wave smashed into her. The rope jerked taut.

Treading water, she looked back. A log had caught the rope. It rolled, wedged into the ceiling, and the line went tight like a trap.

Mari swung on the rope as the current dragged her downstream. Another wave broke over her. Mud filled her mouth. Something solid struck her under the surface and knocked the breath from her chest.

Mari fought up and gasped.

The far pup slid past along the distant shore.

Behind her, a high-pitched cry cut through the roar of water. Mari whipped around and threw out an arm, catching the nearer pup by its scruff. Tiny paws clung to her soaked fur. She fought her way back toward the log where the rope had snagged. It had only looped once, and she managed to free it with numb digits.

Her father and Phlip towed her and the pup back to the near shore. They used the fence to haul her over.

Mari collapsed to her knees, panting and coughing as water spilled from her lungs. "I couldn't save them both," she choked out, eyes welling. "Dad… the other one was too far."

Her father pulled her into a hug before she could say more, sandwiching the pup between them. "You did amazing," he said, voice rough. "Your mother would be so proud."

The three of them climbed back onto Phlip. Mari wiped the drying muck from her face, took the reins, and steadied her voice.

"Go, Phlip. Get us out of here."

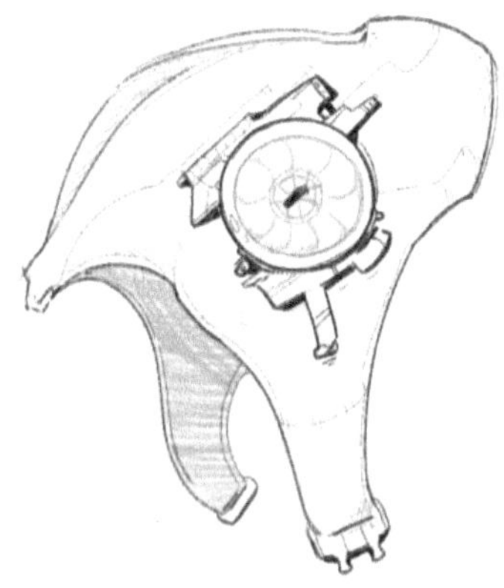

CHAPTER 3 | DEEPWORKS

Rushing water encapsulated Jerro. The current formed a sphere that warped around him, accompanied by a low, oscillating hum that shifted with his movement. He approached a long control panel nested among an array of pipes and gauges.

From the torrent, another sphere merged with his.

"Keeper Aleese, I don't think we can close the breach from the control room. But I can triage the damage," Jerro said, forcing his voice over the roar.

"Good thinking, Cog Wavetail," the Keeper said, calm as ever. "Define the problem. Then solve it. Just as you trained in Builders Basic."

Jerro restrained a smile. He pulled up a series of holographic displays and began moving his paws, engaging the translucent interface. He toggled a set of ribbon sliders into position, then flipped through feeds, grabbing them with a paw and tossing them aside.

"Keeper, if I perform an emergency closure on access tunnels thirteen through twenty, I think we can slow the flooding."

On a fresh display, the Deepworks schematic bloomed to life. The Keeper spun it from a side profile to a bird's-eye plan view. She zoomed in to inspect the specified tunnels. "Agreed. We can also reduce sluice gate two-alpha to ten percent."

Green switches clicked beneath Jerro's paw, one by one, then bled to red. The Keeper spun a dial back with one paw while using her other to steady the display, monitoring the gate's flow rate.

"This won't stop it." The Keeper kept the dial steady. "But it buys the emergency team time."

"What do you think caused this?" Jerro asked.

"I'm not sure." The Keeper's eyes hardened. "Pull the feeds back up."

With a spread of his paws, Jerro slid the displays back into alignment. He returned to scanning the various locations throughout Deepworks.

"There." The Keeper pointed at one of the four displays, halting Jerro's progress.

Three dark-cloaked figures moved hurriedly down a pipe-lined corridor.

Jerro fixated on the screen. "This wasn't an accident."

"I'd bet a thousand greens it wasn't. In all my years, I've never seen damage like this from a malfunction." The Keeper paused, then pointed to the bottom left display as the three obscured shapes entered from the left and moved through a round tunnel lined with parallel piping.

"That tunnel leads straight to Turbine Gallery II." She pointed at the display. "We're closer than any response team. Call it in as we move."

Lockers lined the wall. She went straight for them and pulled out two large metallic discs. After giving them a rhythmic tap, they sprang to life, hovering half a tail above the ground. She jumped onto one without hesitation.

Jerro stepped onto the other. His webbed foot slipped off the edge, and he ended up mounting the platform belly first, then spun his lower body around and found his footing. The Keeper watched him maneuver his pear-shaped body into place.

A patient, flat-lipped smile tugged at her mouth. "Ready, Cog Wavetail?"

"Affirmative, Keeper," Jerro said, standing upright.

With their acoustic spheres shielding them from the torrent, they shot down the arched passage where the flow had subsided.

"What if they reach the turbines first?" Jerro asked as they swept through a long straight section. "What if they do more damage?"

"Call it in to third shift. Stay on my tail. I'll notify Ordinate Rull. We need backup," the Keeper said, glancing back at him.

Jerro braced a paw against his temple and formed a mental link. "Third shift notified."

They sped through the tunnels, making quick work of a route they knew by heart.

A pale figure lay motionless across the corridor ahead, ghost-white, damp fur plastered to its body. Webbed feet trailed in the stream of water rippling down the center. A long, ratlike tail was wrenched into a horrific knot, limbs frozen in contorted poses.

"Keeper…" Jerro's voice caught. "A nutria sentinel. What happened to her?"

The Keeper hopped off her disc and placed a paw to the bleach-white rodent's neck, checking for a pulse. She shook her head slowly. "I don't know, but we're going to find out."

Her eyes hardened. "She's gone. I'll report it to the Ordinate. We keep moving."

They were nearing the location from the holographic feed.

"We're getting close," the Keeper said. "Stay vigilant now."

Jerro shifted his webbed feet and tried to turn his disc to check behind them. His balance faltered, and he aborted the movement. He closed his eyes and placed a paw on his temple again.

The Keeper turned her head over her shoulder. "No pulse scan. I already ran one. Nothing behind us. Save your energy."

"Affirmative, Keeper."

A circular doorway marked the end of the tunnel. TURBINE GALLERY II was stenciled above it in blocky white letters. They stepped off and deactivated the hovering discs. Jerro managed it cleanly this time.

The door was propped open by a locking bar that hadn't been reengaged. This part of Deepworks was dry, aside from minor leaks that pinged occasionally as intermittent drops fell from old fittings.

With Jerro on her tail, the Keeper slowly pushed the door open.

They entered a long room with high ceilings packed with repeating half-cylinders emerging from the floor and robust pipework winding throughout. Rectangular units spanned the far wall, generating a roaring hum that vibrated in Jerro's teeth.

The Keeper looked at Jerro, and without moving her mouth, communicated a feeling into his mind.

Stay quiet and stay close.

Jerro's mouth tightened and he nodded.

They wove through the vibrating metal maze. As they moved deeper, distant chatter emerged through the white noise. High-pitched squeaks followed. A short, throaty shriek faded. Then a round of screeches.

The Keeper glanced back at Jerro, eyes narrowed. Jerro lifted his paws in a helpless, questioning gesture.

A faint blood-red glow bled through gaps in the machinery ahead, casting shadowed movement across the near wall.

Before they could catch a clear glimpse, a deep guttural voice stopped them in their tracks.

They froze, stacking tight against the side of the nearest purring turbine. The Keeper flipped down a transparent monocular eyepiece. Jerro followed.

With swift, tactical precision, they moved around the corner, paw to temple, the other outstretched and facing forward.

The three figures they had seen on the monitors were suspended midair. Their cloak hoods had fallen back, exposing stout furry heads with pointed snouts. Their bodies were contorted, arms and legs shifting in grotesque configurations.

At the center, the source of the blood-red light revealed itself.

Filaments of energy were being drawn from the smaller members of the formation, funneling into a coalescing crimson gyre. At its focal point stood a larger, heavily muscled version of its smaller counterparts. Smoothly wielding sharp claws, the behemoth gestured with practiced control, shaping the vortex.

A maniacal smile anchored its vicious nose and sallow, sunken porcelain eyes.

What stood out to Jerro, though, were the teeth. Fangs—the kind you'd see on big cats or other predators—protruded down and out of its wicked mouth.

Jerro and the Keeper froze, stupefied by the stage of alien information that had penetrated their familiar world. The larger creature's focus shifted. Its smile faded into a devilish glare as its gaze locked onto the Keeper.

Her eyes rolled back, whites exposed. She burrowed into the mind of the beast, her outstretched paw grasping at blank air.

Jerro felt it like a sledgehammer. A wave of nausea and a splitting headache overwhelmed him and drove him to his knees. He looked to the Keeper for help, only to realize he was merely collateral.

Keeper Aleese doubled over and released a shuddering scream that echoed through the gallery.

Sanguine coils of energy formed between them, flowing away from her and into the brute. The three smaller creatures dropped to the ground and squirmed. The Keeper lifted into the air, drawn toward the hulking, vampiric form.

The villain laughed, deep and vengeful. The sound hit Jerro with the explosiveness of a shockwave.

Jerro's eyes darted, searching for anything that might help. Generators. Ceiling. Turbines.

The brute stood on a large pad marked by nested triangles forming a nine-point star. Thick tentacles connected the pad to the machinery. Heavy cables expanded and shrank like a flexible straw, drawing down a thick substance. As the engorged section moved from turbine to platform, it released a deep orange glow that high-lighted the veiny structure.

Jerro's monocular caught an anomaly along the sidewall of a pipe. A blue waveform pulsed across his eyepiece. High pressure. Routing into the turbine.

The corrupted growth had spread finger-like roots along the pipework, compromising the structure.

Helplessness fell away, and his jaw set.

Jerro focused on the water within the pipe. He manipulated it into a zone of pressure that induced powerful shockwaves. The pipe shook violently and began to hammer, every molecule straining for release.

The pipe erupted.

A rush of water inundated the creatures, knocking down the two nearest the rupture. Jerro's posture now mimicked the Keeper's, paw to temple, the other outstretched.

He turned his attention to the smaller creatures and targeted the only one still on its feet.

Jerro reached into its mind.

It was chaotic, full of malice and hate like he had never felt before, as if that was its only purpose. He saw flashes of a dark landscape beneath a deep maroon skyline. The creature flew on a widewinged, stark gray bird with a thick bill.

The scene jumped.

Another, smaller member of its kind embraced it. Love. Comfort. The contrast hit Jerro so hard it nearly pulled him under. Malice and warmth braided together in a way his mind struggled to hold.

Jerro's eyes softened. His mouth loosened as he tried to find a weakness, to mold its mind to his bidding.

Then nothing.

He looked up.

The creature was gone, leaving only a fading red mist where it had stood. With a grin, the pale giant pointed a blade finger at the empty space. Behind their master, the other two squeaked and rushed for cover.

Jerro saw them reach into a small bag and pull out a hollow metal hoop. They expanded it to the size of a wide doorway and threw it at the far wall, where it adhered.

From the smooth circumference, black liquid filled the ring, wavering like the surface of a raging ocean. It lapped out, sucked back, then calmed to modest peaks.

Jerro's vision snapped back to the Keeper.

She was being drawn within touch of the demon. The smooth brown of her coat went coarse and stark as she neared it. Her body withered and thinned, anemic, like an old apple core left to rot in the desert. Even her strong paddle tail dangled limp.

All the while, the color of the demon deepened, its coat turning a shade of burnt charcoal.

Jerro shook his head and gritted his teeth. His feet carried him forward without consent. He charged, terror burning behind his eyes, and unleashed his fiercest battle cry.

One of the smaller monsters stepped out from behind the pale beast and lifted a paw at Jerro.

Jerro became weightless.

His momentum inverted. He flew backward across the room, slamming into the wall.

Deepworks reasserted itself. Jerro sucked in a wet, choking breath. The blood-red glow was gone, replaced by familiar blue lighting. The rhythmic hum of the generators dominated again.

Jerro tried to stand and collapsed to his side against the cool, damp stone. A biting headache flared as his senses sharpened. Propping himself with his right arm, he involuntarily opened his mouth and released a stream of bile that pooled and ran back toward him.

He looked down.

A white, jagged stick protruded from his blood-soaked fur.

Jerro scanned the room. In the distance lay a disheveled, stark-white pile.

Arm over arm, he dragged his broken body across the gritty floor, stopping every few pulls to grimace and catch his breath. When he reached the withered lump, he grasped the side and rolled it over.

"Keeper," he choked out, scrambling for a pulse.

She was still. Opaque white marbles sat in her sockets. Drying blood streaked from the corners of her eyes. Matching streams ran from her nose and ears.

Jerro lay beside her for a moment.

Then he heard the approaching slaps of webbed feet down the gallery.

"We're over here!" he yelled, voice cracking. "Help her!"

A series of thin-tailed nutria sentinels rushed into the space between the turbines where the battle had unfolded.

An aged, graying sentinel knelt beside Jerro and placed a paw on his chest, assessing his vitals. "You're gonna be okay, pup."

Jerro reached toward the Keeper. "What about her?"

Another light-brown sentinel knelt by the Keeper, lips pursed flat. She squinted, then shook her head.

Jerro's vision narrowed. Darkness worked in from the edges. He turned his head and saw a rotund beaver approach with a twisted cane. A scar crossed his silver face, cutting over a patched eye.

"Ordinate Rull," a sentinel said. "Keeper Aleese is gone. This Cog needs medical. Now."

Muffled chatter filled the turbine gallery. Jerro's vision collapsed to a pinpoint as he was lifted off the gritty surface.

44

CHAPTER 4 | WORM

A jet-black mat spread across the floor, leaving only a thin border of stone exposed. White line work marked the battle ring, a circle bisected cleanly in half. Centered in each half sat a small white box, and within each box stood a stout rodent in black robes trimmed in white with red accents. Around them, smaller cross-legged versions of the two combatants watched in matching uniforms. Young marmots and prairie dogs, still and intent.

One figure broke the symmetry. A larger marmot, graying at the muzzle, wore inverted robes, white with black trim.

Above, glowing rock traced arched columns that met at the dome's apex. Opposing doors waited in the stone walls. Along the perimeter, incense braziers burned, steeping the room in cedar and honeysuckle. Smoke climbed, pooled near the crown, and bled away through hidden vents.

In the ring, the combatants faced each other and bowed.

The elder marmot stepped onto the mat. His robes flowed with each careful stride, revealing a mechanical leg of tiny gears and pistons working with fluid precision, though it did little to smooth the rough hobble. Age bent him forward, kyphotic, the hump beneath his robes rounding his upper back.

"Young masters," he said, smile quivering. His voice wavered, yet projected well in the diffuse acoustics. "This is the final round of the sixty-seventh Psy Trial. Master Jake and Master Greg will demonstrate the full martial prowess of a burrowing rodent trained in the Way of the Earthshaker."

"The rocks remember!" shouted the youthful warriors lining the ring in unison. The elder marmot's grin widened, yellowed teeth showing.

He eyed each of the combatants, then turned toward them shakily. "Masters, are you ready?"

They nodded.

"Take form!"

Jake and Greg assumed different starting positions. Jake took a staggered stance, arms forward, paws open. Greg spread his feet wide, paws clenched into fists and tucked tight to his waist.

The gym went dead silent. Embers crackled in the braziers.

"Initiate," the old marmot commanded, firm but hushed. He took three quick steps back, smooth and calculated, a stark contrast to his earlier hobble.

Jake burst forward.

Greg shifted a fraction to the side, letting the strike skim past, then countered. Jake read it. Their forearms collided and locked. They pushed, neither giving an inch.

Something else met between them.

Two immovable wills, not quite thoughts laid open, more like pressure where their minds pressed together. Bodies braced. Breath held. At the edges of mindspace, a shallow contact strained, searching.

And Jake found the seam.

Not a memory taken, just an echo that slipped loose in the struggle. Greg's father. A long line of Gregs. Disappointment set like stone. The fear of never living up to the name.

Jake hooked it and pulled.

Inadequacy surged to the surface. Greg faltered, eyes narrowing, face twisting. The lock broke at once, physical and mental, and the emotion snapped outward as a shockwave that shoved them apart.

Jake didn't waste the gap. He joined his paws at the wrist, palms out, and drove a concentrated burst at Greg.

Around the ring, the novices moved together. Open-pawed—shielding. A translucent dome snapped into place.

Greg threw up his own shield, smaller but sharp. The impact drove him back, paws skidding along the mat. His barrier deflected most of the force upward, where it splashed against the larger dome and scattered into a prismatic shimmer.

Greg refocused, angry at his weakness, furious that Jake had seen it.

Not quick enough.

Jake smirked and closed the distance, snapping a perfectly formed Earthshaker Pawstrike that sent Greg reeling into the force field.

Jake stayed on him. He had the fight, and they both knew it. Doubt flooded Greg's mind as Jake moved for the submission. Greg defended, but he was hurt. His maneuvers slowed. Jake read every choice before it happened.

Jake's grin widened, eyes glinting, as he wrestled Greg down and cinched in a chokehold.

Greg bucked and strained, nose pressed into Jake's stubby forearm. He tried to wedge a finger into the gap, but Jake's arm bulged tighter, like a predator pinning prey under its weight.

Greg tapped the mat, rapid and desperate.

The old marmot ended it. Jake, victor. Greg, defeated.

As Greg stood and straightened his robes, he felt the room before he saw it. The circle of novices leaned toward each other, murmuring in hushed whispers. For over a century, the line of Greg had held the title of Archpsy.

Not today.

Today it returned to the line of Jake.

Greg's body moved as if running a routine program. He returned to his starting block, bowed out with Jake, and exited the ring. Behind him, commotion and celebration swelled as he left the chamber.

"Yeah. I am a disappointment," Greg muttered, slipping into the dingy gear room.

He grabbed his bag from an earthen cubby and changed into civilian attire with quick, solemn movements. Fabric and buckles whispered. His locker thudded shut. Every so often, cheers seeped through the walls like mockery.

Greg paused at the door and looked back into the familiar space. His brow furrowed, then he dropped his gaze and turned away.

The hall to the main entrance was lined with portraits, each titled Greg. His father. His grandfather. His great-grandfather. Names that weren't names so much as expectations. He walked until there were no more.

He left the Earthshaker Gym, the first major expansion of The Burrow, carved nearly two thousand cycles ago. A colossal stone carving of a proud prairie dog towered over the entrance. Greg approached the monument and read the placard.

THE FIRST ARCHPSY AND THE LAST IN THE LINE OF CHUCK.

SEED OF A NEW ERA.

MAY THE MEMORY OF HIS SACRIFICE NEVER BE BURIED.

Greg placed a paw on the plaque and looked up at the looming statue. His eyes glazed as his stare tunneled through the carved face as though staring hard enough could change what had already happened. He lingered on the word *sacrifice*, tracing the groove of the cut letters.

He drifted through The Spine on his way home. The world narrowed to a smear of stone and motion.

"Greg!"

A voice called again and again, pulling his mind back into place. Emergency tones echoed through the chasm. The damp chill of wet earth rose through his fur.

Greg glanced over his shoulder—uncertain that the call was meant for him at all.

He blinked and saw her. Mari mounted on Phlip's back. Her father rode behind, arms locked tight. The pup was wedged safely between them.

"What are you doing here?" Mari asked.

Like he had just arrived, Greg took in the scene around him.

Hundreds of drenched and displaced rodents slogged through debris-laden streets, gathering into small groups. A baby mouse sat in the mud crying out until a family of moles stopped, the mother scooping it up tight and quelling the tears. Nearby, a corpulent rat dug through sludge with frantic paws, sending chunks flying. It pulled free a footlocker caked in wet soil and scurried off.

"Mari... what's happening?" Greg's voice barely cleared his throat. He stared at the soggy inhabitants and washed-out passages leading to various digs.

"There was a breach at Deepworks," Mari said, scanning the diminished flows trickling down the digs and spilling in small waterfalls into the pit. At its center, The Spine's crystal structure rose vertically, catching the runoff in pale glints. "But the water's slowing. For now, at least."

The crystal shuddered. Its light faded.

Gasps filled The Spine, echoing upward. The crystal flickered, then steadied into its daybreak yellow.

Mari and Greg looked at each other again. Mari's brow furrowed above deep brown eyes. "Have you seen Jerro?"

"He was on shift this lune," Greg said, half question, half statement.

"Go check on your friend," Mari's dad said, sliding off Phlip. "I'll stay here and help."

Greg stepped closer and wrapped Mari's dad in a hug, bending down to meet the smaller gopher. "Seriously, you're the best, Mr. Stonepaw."

"For the thousandth time, call me by my first name," Mari's dad groaned, patting his back.

Greg caught Mari's eyes and mouthed a question. She couldn't make it out, but produced an agreeable shrug anyway, playing along.

"You got it, Jupi," Greg said, grinning from far above Jupi's head.

Mari hopped off Phlip and hugged her dad tight. He kissed the top of her head. "You did great, kiddo. Now go find Jerro and make sure he's okay."

They split paths.

Jupi set off to aid his fellow denizens, guiding the Graslow pup by the paw. Greg, Mari, and Phlip pushed up the main dig that led toward Deepworks.

The route was ruined. Flood debris and mud coated everything, smothering the bioluminescent roots. Only the higher stretches still shone. They picked their way through the slop, paws suctioning, balance never quite certain.

From Phlip's back, Mari watched Greg. He moved like a machine, head down, driving through it. When a circular door wedged in the mud blocked their path, he tore it free with a shout, cracked it over his head, and hurled the pieces down the dig.

Mari pulled Phlip's reins to stop. "Greg, what's going on with you?"

"Just living up to my father's disappointment," Greg said flatly. "So, nothing new."

Mari swung down into the mud and slogged to him. She put a paw on his arm, as high as she could reach. "You're an amazing marmot. You're one of the strongest, most dedicated rodents in this Burrow."

"Thanks, Mari." His eyes stayed down. "I wish my father felt the same. Doesn't matter now."

"What do you mean, it doesn't matter?"

"I lost the title. Jake crushed me. My father will never forgive me for failing the lineage." Greg shook his head, pulled away, and kept moving.

Mari hopped back onto Phlip and caught up. "Greg, your father is a fool if he doesn't believe in you."

"I've given him every reason in the world not to."

They walked on in silence, broken only by the suction of their feet pulling free. Every so often, a faint tremor shivered through the packed earth, loosening mud from the roots.

"Greg, something strange happened to me—"

"Stop," Greg said, cutting her off.

Mari shot him a glare.

Then Greg's face shifted. "Wait," he breathed. "Do you feel that?"

Mari pressed a paw to Phlip's ear. Phlip sank low to the ground without a sound. Mari slid off the saddle, taking care not to make a sound.

A low rumble began and steadily built.

"It's coming at us," Mari muttered.

Down the dig, it came into view. A huge pulsating mass filled the passage, hurtling toward them, crushing debris and extinguishing the last of the bioluminescence as it wriggled forward. The head, if you could call it that, emerged. Enormous spikes protruded around a beak-like mouth lined with razor-sharp teeth.

Mari yanked the petrified watermelon helmet from her bag. "I've got a plan. We've only got one shot. Get on my tail and direct a blast at me!" she yelled over the rising roar.

Greg stumbled behind her as the ground quaked underfoot.

The creature closed in. One hundred tails. Eighty. Sixty.

It was moving impossibly fast.

"Now!" Mari shouted.

No response.

"Greg. Now!" She looked back over her shoulder.

He was frozen.

Mari took two quick steps back, grabbed a tuft of his chest fur, and jumped to smack his face. "Greg, I need you." Her voice went hard. "Focus on me."

The daze broke.

Greg lifted his paws and formed the open-pawed gesture around his body, finishing with a flourish toward Mari. Mari was already moving. She harnessed the momentum of Greg's blast and rotated it around herself in perfect form as the beast's gaping maw bore down.

Darkness engulfed everything.

Then warmth.

The air filled with a musky bouquet of damp earth and decaying foliage, followed by a sharp fishy note.

Mari flicked on her lantern and turned toward Greg.

Greg stood perfectly still, completely covered in chunks of flesh and unknown goop. He stared at Mari. Then they both turned toward Phlip.

Phlip's tongue smacked into Mari like a wet towel. His eyes widened. He started hacking and sneezing, then sat back on his hind legs and tried to scrub the taste from his mouth with muddy paws. It only made things worse.

"Aw gross," Mari said to Phlip. "Why would you do that?"

Greg let out a laugh, the sound cracking his dour mood. Mari joined in, and for a moment they reveled in the near-death triumph.

"We did it," Greg shouted. "No one is going to believe we just defeated a worm!"

"It doesn't matter what anyone believes," Mari said, smiling. "We know it."

Greg held his paws up, then down low. Mari jumped and smacked both. He scooped her up and swung her in a circle, then plopped her down beside Phlip, who hopped in place, matching their energy.

After a few moments, they gathered themselves and wiped off the worst of it. Greg led the way, blasting a path through the worm's soft lining.

They pushed on through the slick tunnel toward Deepworks.

CHAPTER 5 | REUNION

A bright light hovered over Jerro, engulfing his view. Rodents in medical scrubs rotated into the edges of his narrowed vision. Metal instruments clattered while the team spoke in serious, clipped tones, calling out their every move. Jerro drew a deep breath of latex and iodine before a mask covered his face and the smell was replaced by an acrid sting.

"Keeper… is she…" His voice trailed off under the mask.

Darkness took him again.

Jerro opened his eyes slowly. Sticky dryness tugged at his lips. Bile coated his tongue, and he swallowed hard, forcing it down. The room was sterile, but not cold. One door faced him. A smoky window was set three quarters of the way up. Packed earthen walls held their shape, smooth and clean. Glowing mushrooms pooled soft light along the edges, and a simple metal lamp on the bedside table cast a warm downlight across his blankets.

His mind drifted briefly to Builders Basic. The peanut incident. A group of Cogs had slipped peanuts into his lunch, convinced it would be funny.

"It wasn't funny," he muttered.

His face tightened, then the memory let go and the reason he was here rushed back in.

Jerro reached down to feel his leg. The bone wasn't sticking out anymore. It wasn't cast or secured, just wrapped in a simple bandage around his upper leg. The area was sore, and he could feel lumps beneath the wrap. His head was wrapped too, in a thick band that felt cool to the touch.

A shadow crossed the window, and a quick knock followed. Before he could answer, the door opened.

A beaver entered wearing an open, long white coat. She carried a pad tucked under her arm. A mask hung under her chin, and a colorful headband held back her fur. It was hard to tell, but she looked little older than Jerro.

"Good late lune. Or is it morning?" She smiled faintly at her pad. "I've lost track. My name is Doctor Mossbank. I performed your surgery, and I'm overseeing your recovery."

"What happened to Keeper Aleese?" Jerro asked.

The doctor's smile faded. She pulled a chair from the corner and sat at his bedside.

"I'm afraid she didn't make it. I'm sorry." She paused and then spoke gently, as if she were placing each word where it belonged. "She was gone before she reached us."

Jerro looked away and fought the knot forming in his throat. "What happens next?"

The doctor shifted upright, pad resting on her lap. "Once I clear you to return to duty, you'll be back in the paws of The Builders. From there…" She exhaled. "That's out of my domain."

Jerro kept his gaze fixed on the wall, holding his expression still.

"Let me see that leg," she said, patting the mattress beside his injured thigh.

Jerro propped himself up on the pillows. "Wasn't it broken? Why isn't it cast?"

"No… Well, yes." She smiled, like she'd been waiting for that one. "Yes, it was broken. No, we didn't use a cast. You're the newest recipient of a novel tech from the Burrow Health Institute. Nanomites."

Jerro blinked. "That's cool. What exactly are nanomites?"

Doctor Mossbank tapped her pad and lifted it. A diagram of a tiny robot filled the screen.

"Miniscule inorganic machines. We injected them after I reset your leg and put everything back where it should be. By now they should've rebuilt the bone lattice and are currently speeding up tissue regeneration." Her eyes brightened. "Let's look."

She gently lifted his bandaged leg and began unwrapping it.

The door swung open without warning.

Ordinate Rull entered, accompanied by a nutria sentinel who stood guard.

"Cog Jerro," the Ordinate said roughly, then cleared his throat. "I'm glad you're awake. I have a few questions regarding your encounter."

Jerro sat straighter against the headboard. "Of course, Ordinate."

Rull turned slightly toward the doctor. "How's he recovering? I heard you used the new nanomite tech."

Doctor Mossbank inspected Jerro's bare leg. The spot where the bone had protruded was already closed.

"Amazing," she murmured, more to herself than anyone.

She bent his leg and guided it through its full range of motion. "How does that feel? Any pain?"

"It's a little sore," Jerro said, surprised by his own smile. "But no pain."

The doctor beamed and glanced at the monitor on the wall behind him. "Vitals look great. I'm going to recommend discharge. Take it easy on that new bone for a lune or two and come back for your follow-up. We want to record the progress and make sure you don't need additional treatment."

She removed the sensors, one from his forehead and another from his finger, then unwrapped the bandage on his head.

"Your gear should be in this cabinet," she said, opening a small door against the far wall to show him. "Oh, and the nanomites will break down after about ten lunes. Your body will take care of the rest from there."

Ordinate Rull shuffled to the bedside chair and took the seat the doctor had been using. "Thanks for putting him back together, Doctor."

She nodded and headed for the door. The nutria sentinel opened it for her. "Of course. And sorry to move your Cog out so quickly. As you know, we're short on beds."

"Understood, doctor. Thank you for your concern," the Ordinate replied.

The latch clicked.

He rested his gnarled cane between his legs and stacked both paws on its end. He did not take his one good eye off Jerro. "Sentinel, leave us."

The nutria obeyed. The door closed again.

"Tell me, Cog," the Ordinate said, voice low. "What happened down there?"

Jerro explained what he could, working through the ordeal in the order his mind would allow. Their attempt to slow the flooding. The cloaked creatures. The dead sentinel. The turbine gallery. Keeper Aleese.

"Can you tell me where they went?" Ordinate Rull asked.

"I have no idea," Jerro said. "They had this hoop thing."

"What did it look like?"

"They put it on the wall, and it filled with black liquid. Like a thick ocean. Like a lake of oil." Jerro swallowed. "I don't remember much after that. I think I was knocked unconscious, then the sentinels showed up."

Ordinate Rull sat back and frowned. After a moment, he shifted his weight and stood. "This stays between us. For now."

Jerro's throat tightened. "What am I supposed to do now?"

"I'm placing you on medical leave until you're cleared at your follow-up. Go home and get some rest." The Ordinate's voice softened just slightly. "You and the Keeper's bravery were exemplary of The Builder code."

Jerro stared at the blanket, focus slipping. "Keeper Aleese…"

"She was a hero to The Burrow and our order," Ordinate Rull said. "She will be posthumously awarded the Builder's Timber Cross."

Jerro's eyelids dammed the tears. He shifted on the bed, trying to breathe past the pressure in his chest. "Her kits," Jerro said, staring at the blanket. "She had two. They'll grow up without her."

The Ordinate reached a paw to Jerro's. "In Deepworks, you learn quickly," he said, thumb pressing once into Jerro's paw, "you can't save everything." He held Jerro's eyes. "You know how that goes as well as anyone. We'll make sure her kits are taken care of. That is what we can do."

He hobbled to the door, then turned back and rendered a salute. Jerro returned it from the bed, quick and unsteady. The Ordinate exited.

Jerro waited only long enough for the latch to settle before swinging his legs over the side. He reached for his issued jacket, and his paw betrayed him, a fine tremor he couldn't still. The Keeper's eyes flashed up, glassy and wrong.

He pushed through the feeling, whispering the eulogy of The Burrow to himself. "We burrow."

With a deep breath, his paw steadied. Jerro snatched his gear, shoved his way into the hall, and dropped his transit disc. The tunnels blurred as he took off.

He swept into a marble-lined antechamber where gray and black swirls climbed into shadow. A long glossy counter ran the length of the wall, tucked beneath a cantilevered recess. Velvet ropes marked an empty queue, and holoscreens behind the desks looped

Deepworks history for visiting citizens. A recorded voice drifted through hidden speakers, cheerful and neutral, the kind meant for tours.

"The Builders trace their history back as far as The Folding, a time before recorded history…"

The vestibule felt hushed in that polished way, all echo and distance, until a sudden pounding cut through it. Beyond the semi-transparent doors, two large silhouettes and a smaller one hammered at the barrier, shouting over one another. Their words came through as dull, swallowed syllables.

The sentinel on the left turned and yelled toward them. "We already told you, no one gets in. Facility is locked down by order of the Ordinate."

Jerro dismounted carefully, sitting and swinging his legs to the floor. The sentinel on the right, dark brown fur slicked flat, nodded at the pad. "If you've got orders, scan out. Things are especially tight right now."

"The Ordinate cleared me, should be in system," Jerro said, placing his paw on the adjacent pad. A soft red glow lit beneath his skin, then flipped to green with a swift positive tone. He looked towards the doors. "Who's out there?"

The sentinel shrugged. "A little gopher and the biggest, grumpiest marmot I've ever seen. Said they're checking on a friend. But…" He lifted his paws. "Lockdown."

Jerro's eyes lit, and a grin broke through his exhaustion. "Oh. I may be able to resolve this situation for you guys."

The guard straightened and rendered a sharp salute. Jerro returned it with less formality and strolled through the doors.

The Builders' crest flanked the entrance to Deepworks on two enormous banners. A black circle with a white triangle overlaid, and centered within them, an engineer's hammer.

On one side of the foyer stood a copper bust of the first Ordinate. On the other, a wall-sized illustration depicted the original construction of Deepworks.

Jerro pushed open one of the massive doors leading to the stepped entrance.

"Jerro!" Mari shouted. She sprang up from the top step where she had been sitting and wrapped her short arms around him as far as she could reach.

Greg approached with a tired smile as Jerro and Mari broke their hug. He and Jerro placed a paw on each other's opposing shoulders.

"It's good to see you both," Jerro said. Then his nose wrinkled. "Why do you smell so bad?"

"And Phlip," Jerro added, just as Phlip bounded forward and knocked him to the ground, nuzzling his giant floppy face into Jerro's.

"Alright, alright," Jerro laughed, struggling under the rabbit's enthusiasm. "That's enough, you big ball of fur."

He pushed his way up finally, and the four of them started back down the dig together.

"Mari, don't you have a trial coming up?" Jerro asked.

"Yeah. I wanted to ask you about that, actually." Mari's voice shifted. "We were at Tailweaver's earlier. How long ago was that?"

Jerro narrowed his eyes. "Before my shift. Maybe ten or twelve hours ago. Don't you remember?"

"I do," Mari said. "But that was the last thing I remember before waking up in an old ruined cave on the north end of Long Valley."

"What?" Greg cut in, louder than he meant to. "You were out of The Burrow again?"

"Yeah," Mari said. "But I don't remember how I got there."

Jerro glanced at her, serious now, as they passed a collapsed section of the dig wall. "Unsanctioned excursions are forbidden, Mari. You're going to get in trouble one of these times."

"Jerro, I know you don't approve, but this is different. I have no idea how I ended up out there. Don't you think that's odd?"

Jerro stopped and paced in front of her. Mari rolled her eyes and waited him out.

"It is," Jerro admitted. "And maybe that's the point. Beyond the birds, there are anomalies on the surface." He paused. "Rufus might know something. He hoards old history and ancient tech like it's treasure."

"That's what I was thinking," Mari said. "I stopped by Tail-weavers when I got back, but he wasn't around."

Jerro turned his attention back to the breach in the dig wall. "This is worse than I thought," he said, looking over the damage and then down the muddied tunnel. Debris was scattered and embedded in drying muck.

Then his gaze snagged on something else.

Chunks of worm flesh decorated the periphery.

Jerro pointed at a hunk of jellied tissue. "What's all this?"

"Oh yeah," Greg said without slowing. "We killed an earthworm." He dropped to all fours and took off ahead, leaving Jerro and Mari behind.

"Yeah," Mari called after him. She lowered her voice and focused her attention on Jerro. "It was pretty cool. And also likely why we smell bad."

Jerro blinked, then hurried to keep pace with Mari and Phlip. "Must have been drawn to the water," he said. "How exactly did you do that?"

"Honestly, I'm not sure," Mari said. "I think it was mostly Greg's psionics, not mine. But I used a duo technique Mister Craghorb had been teaching. That was the first time I got it to work."

Jerro gave her a look that held both surprise and respect. "I'm impressed. Even the sentinels have a hard time taking down errant worms."

They pushed on toward The Spine. Mari rode Phlip. Jerro skimmed low on his disc. Greg surged ahead through the rough patches, stopping only long enough for them to catch up, impatience carved into every glance.

Blue light spilled around the last bend. The crystal's glow steadied into its familiar daybreak hue.

The plaza was crowded and half-turned into a relief camp. Bedrolls and makeshift awnings hugged the walls. Sentinels and medical teams moved through the churn, hauling, lifting, guiding the dazed toward triage. A throng of citizens pressed toward a white-columned building with blunt capitals carved across the lintel. THE BANK OF THE BURROW.

Near the edge of the crowd, Mari spotted her dad speaking with two others she recognized from the war. Another gopher, broader than Jupi, with mechanical forearms that whirred softly as he pointed toward the empty podium. Beside him, a ground squirrel turned, and patches of fur gave way to smooth swirls of scarred skin.

Mari backed a few steps toward Greg and Jerro. "I'm going to check in with my dad real quick. See what's going on."

"Sounds good," Greg said, voice flattening again. He nodded toward a massive marmot ringed by followers in small black cylinder hats. "I'll just stay here. I'm not ready for that conversation."

"I'll stay too," Jerro said. His gaze swept the crowd. "No beavers. No riding rabbits." He nudged Phlip with an elbow and managed a faint smile. "You can babysit us."

Mari slipped into the gaps and surfaced beside Jupi.

"Hey, Dad."

He turned, startled, then softened. "Oh, hey my little carrot." He pulled her into a tight hug. "Did you and Greg find Jerro?"

"Yeah," Mari said. "He's okay. Well, mostly." She pointed back through the crowd.

Jerro and Phlip were circling Greg in a clumsy little game of tag. Greg sat still as stone, enduring it like a punishment.

"What's going on?" Mari asked.

"Councilmember Kaet came out," Jupi said. "They're setting up ration distribution for displaced citizens. Repair plans too. The head banker is opening reserve stockpiles." He glanced toward the podium, still empty, then back to her.

The words had barely landed before a coughing fit folded him. He excused himself and staggered out of the crowd, doubling over. Mari followed, rubbing his bony back, tracing each rib until the attack passed.

Jupi wiped a tear left over from the struggle. A soft smile tried to return, failed, and his mouth set into a straight line as his eyes fixed on Mari.

"Dad?" Mari asked quietly.

"Mari," he said, voice low, "I'm so proud of you. Keep those boys safe. Promise me."

"What?"

"Your friends. No matter what happens." His stare held. Over Mari's shoulder, his eyes flicked once to his old war pals in the crowd, then back, like a silent check-in. "They chose you. And believe it or not, I think they need you now more than ever."

"Dad, are you okay?"

He pulled her into another long hug, then pressed her back with both paws on her shoulders, holding that intense look.

"We love you," he said, fighting back further emotion.

Mari didn't understand, but something in his tone caught in her anyway. They hugged again. "I love you too."

"Alright," Jupi said, and his voice tried to return to normal. "You'd better get going. I'm sure the three of you have a lot to do."

He returned to the crowd. Mari returned to her friends, more confused than she'd been before she went to check in.

∞

Merchant Hollow was quiet. A few vendors were setting up, and a group of young mice took advantage of the empty street. They'd split into two teams for a game of burrow ball.

As the friends passed, a stray ball rolled in front of them. Greg booted it in the opposite direction. The mice stopped their game and watched the ball soar down the desolate corridor.

Mari stared at him. "You could have just kicked it back to them."

"Could have," Greg said plainly.

"I get that you're upset about Jake, but you've got to pull it together."

Jerro blinked. "Wait, what happened?"

"I lost," Greg replied.

Jerro leaned forward, looking around Mari as they walked. "Greg… I'm sorry. Sounds like it's been a rough lune. All around."

They reached the turn leading to Tailweaver's and ducked down the alley. The stained glass was dark. No amber glow from the hearth danced through the windows.

They stopped and looked at each other.

Then Mari stepped forward, placed her paw on the latch, and opened the creaking door into the hushed room.

76

CHAPTER 6 | SUPERPOSITION

The room was devoid of life, and the must of dusty books had reclaimed the air. A cold draft moved along the floor, curling around their paws.

Greg crossed to the hearth and stacked half a dozen chunks of wood on the cool ash. He stared at the pile for a moment, waiting for it to catch on its own, then turned to Mari.

"Have you been able to get your flame yet?"

Mari stepped in beside him and sighed. "I was in the pyrokinetics lab. I made a spark once. Meanwhile, the rest of the class was shooting flamethrowers out of their eyeballs."

Jerro sank into the big corner chair and shut his eyes. Phlip flopped down beside the cold hearth, ears spread like he owned the place.

"I can give it a try, I guess."

She reached toward the wood and focused on the feeling. The emotion of fire. Dancing lights that warmed their den through winter. The rage that reduced everything it touched to ash. Red and yellow energy filled her eyes and licked up toward her brow. A spark fell from her fingertip and fizzled on the wood.

"Just use the lighter," Jerro said, eyes still closed, voice muffled by the upholstery.

Mari threw her paws down and mocked his tone. "Yeah. Just use the lighter, Greg."

She turned toward the short hall, then stopped. Rufus's door was cracked open.

Mari pushed it a little wider, just enough to peer into the shadowed space. A lamp lay knocked over in the far corner, casting its light sideways across the study. The desk was a mess of papers. Drawers had been yanked out and spilled across the floor. Books from Rufus's personal collection lay open, bindings bent back like someone didn't care if they broke.

"Hey, guys…" Mari kept her voice low. "This isn't right."

Behind her, the fire smoldered in the hearth. Mari glanced back over her shoulder.

"Got the fire going," Greg said, then rose to join her.

Jerro lagged behind, chewing on a short bit of wood as he came, the habit doing its best to hold him together.

They stacked at the cracked door, all three peering into the disheveled room.

Mari stepped in first. Greg moved to straighten the fallen lamp. Jerro drifted toward the shelves.

A worn sheet of parchment lay spread across Rufus's desk. One corner was pinned by a bleached white skull with sharp canines. Another by a smooth shard of black stone. Near the edge sat a small glass sphere on a chipped base, cloudy with age, trapping a tiny white house beneath drifting flecks that never quite settled.

Mari pulled the chair upright, careful not to drag it too loudly across the floor. Greg adjusted the lamp so it cast a steadier pool of light. It didn't brighten the entire room, but it gave them enough.

"Looks like a struggle," Jerro said, running a paw over the gouges. He glanced at the heap of books. "Or someone wanted it to look like one."

Mari stepped toward the desk, finding small open islands amid the sea of refuse. "Rufus isn't exactly a neat freak," she said. "But… yeah. I agree."

Greg joined her at the desk. Centered on the parchment was a diagram, three nested triangles forming a star contained in a circle.

"What is it?" he asked.

Mari traced a paw around the central figure without touching it, hovering like she didn't trust what might happen. The symbol webbed into other circles, each holding its own geometric mark, all of it connected by lines that branched and looped like tunnels.

The ink looked thick, almost alive. As her paw passed close, the dark strokes swelled toward her, smoothing beneath her shadow. Mari pulled back fast and flicked her eyes to Greg. "This script…"

Her finger followed the bold symbols across the top. She dropped her pack onto the chair, pulled out the rubbing from the cave, and flattened it beside the parchment. The stacked diamond symbol from her rubbing wasn't on Rufus's diagram, but some of the letters matched well enough to tighten her stomach.

"This is a language," Mari said.

Greg stared at the rubbing. "Where'd that come from?"

"Inside the cave I woke up in," Mari said. "There was more, but most of it was scratched up. I couldn't make it out. I was going to show Rufus and see if he knew anything."

Greg's gaze drifted back over the desk. "Seems like he might. Now we just have to find him."

Jerro joined them, eyes fixed on the parchment. "Wait. I've seen that before."

Mari snapped at him. "Where?"

Jerro hesitated. His jaw worked once, like he was chewing something he didn't want to swallow. "I swore to the Ordinate I wouldn't say anything."

He looked from Mari to Greg, then to Phlip, who had wandered into the study and sat in the corner like a lump of fur pretending he didn't exist.

"You have to promise this stays between us," Jerro said, forcing firmness. "Only us."

Mari straightened and raised an empty paw, like an oath. "Phlip won't say a word. Promise." She held the straight face a beat too long, then a smile slipped out with a small laugh.

Jerro and Greg held steady.

"And neither will we," Greg said. "On our friendship."

Mari nodded, lips pursed, already regretting the laugh.

Jerro drew a breath. "Alright." His eyes searched theirs like he needed traction. "There were creatures in Deepworks."

"What?" Greg and Mari said together.

Mari's expression emptied, the humor wiped clean. "So, it wasn't a failure?"

"Exactly," Jerro said. "They weren't from The Burrow. They weren't anything I've ever seen." His eyes drifted. "They were sinister. You could feel it coming off them. Hate, like it was all they had."

"Jerro, who did this?" Greg asked, trying to anchor him.

Phlip shifted and knocked over a stack of books. He froze, ears up.

"I don't know." Jerro's voice dropped. "They wore cloaks. Moved like they knew the layout. When we finally got to them, there was a larger one and three smaller ones." He swallowed. "It was like they'd grown the larger one somehow. Cables ran into the generators, and when the Keeper and I got there, they resisted our psionics and…"

He stopped, tried again, words catching. "They started doing something to the Keeper. Draining her."

"But you stopped them," Mari said. Hope, thin and shaky.

"No," Jerro swallowed. "Not really." His gaze snapped to the desk like he needed it to keep his place. "I forced a pipe burst. It distracted them. I pushed into the mind of one of the smaller ones, but the big one obliterated it before I could steer it."

He went still, staring into nothing.

Greg's paw returned to Jerro's shoulder. "And then what?"

Jerro blinked and looked at him, eyes driving through Greg instead of at him. "They killed her," he said. "Keeper Aleese." His voice cracked. He blinked hard, looked down, and shoved his face into his elbow to choke back the sound that tried to escape.

"I'm sorry," Greg said. "I didn't know. I was too caught up in my own stuff to even ask."

Mari leaned forward on the desk, voice soft. "We're here for you. You're not alone."

Down the hall, the hearth flared. Firelight flickered once across the doorway.

Jerro shook his head, sniffled, and forced his gaze back to the parchment. "I think they went through some kind of portal. I was knocked out, so I'm not sure." He pointed to the central symbol. "But that mark. That symbol. It was on the floor where the big one was standing."

Greg's brow furrowed. "They knocked you out. Why didn't they kill you too?"

Jerro's paw slid to his leg, almost unconsciously. "I don't know how I survived. They threw me across the room. Probably thought I was dead." He swallowed again. "They had psionics too. Powerful. My leg broke. I passed out. Next thing I remember, doctors." He gave his healed leg a careful smack. "They used experimental regenerative tech."

Mari looked down at the menagerie of symbols and lines. "Jerro… this changes everything. What if this is connected to what happened to me in that cave?"

Before Jerro could answer, the air shifted.

A whisper moved through the room—not words, just motion. Warmth drew out of the space as if a door had opened to winter. A book flipped open on its own. Loose sheets spiraled upward, caught in a tightening whirlwind.

The lamp flickered once, twice, then went out.

Firelight from the hearth should have filled the hall, but it died at the threshold, as though the darkness was drinking it.

Silence pressed down over Tailweaver's.

Then, the heavy front doors creaked open.

Soft footsteps crossed the reading room.

Mari, Greg, and Jerro dropped behind the desk in one motion. Phlip became a statue in the corner, ears lifted, eyes wide and glassy.

They didn't breathe. Not fully.

Mari peered around the side of the desk, exposing only half her face. The footsteps grew closer. A pointed nose broke the line of the doorway, sliding into view. Against the layered shadows of an angular head, a single sharp white fang caught what little light remained.

The head snapped sideways, scanning the study. It paused.

Then the rest of the cloaked body flowed into view.

It looked back down the hall and released a stream of screeches.

Mari withdrew under the desk, pressing tight beside Jerro and Greg.

Cloaks whisked through the room, brushing open books and dragging papers as the figures swept closer. A series of soft thuds hit the floor.

A sweet, grassy stench bloomed in the air.

Mari exhaled a tiny, audible sigh before she could stop it. She knew that smell. Phlip.

The creatures shuffled and screamed again, agitated. Mari tapped her friends and whispered, "We move. Now."

She burst from behind the desk, snatched her helmet from her bag, and jammed it down over her head. Greg split to the other side, moving low and fast. Jerro rose, paw already pressed to his temple.

Three cloaked figures stood in the study, all angled toward Phlip.

Greg hit the nearest one with a full-body tackle, slamming it into the wall beside Phlip. Robes tangled. A hiss of movement. Greg and the creature disappeared into a knot of fabric and limbs.

Jerro's focus locked. The central cloaked figure froze mid-step.

Mari turned toward the shelves, arms extended, palms forward. A pile of books lifted off the shelf in a wobbling cluster, and she sent them across the room in a rough barrage.

The final unaffected creature extended a paw from its sleeve. The books curved away from it and its frozen companion as if repelled by an invisible field. Each near-contact crackled with blood-red energy, arcing and fading in quick ripples.

The creature turned toward Mari and Jerro and clenched the air with its free paw.

Mari's feet lifted.

Jerro's feet lifted.

They were drawn together like gravity had shifted to a single point between them. They slammed and dropped behind the desk in a heap.

Mari's vision blurred. She could see only the ceiling and the edges of the room as Greg was launched upward into it. He stuck for a moment, then dropped, crumbles of shattered earth raining down onto him.

Mari forced herself upright.

The three cloaked figures stood over Greg now, arms outstretched. Blood-red energy began to swirl and stream from their paws.

Mari straightened her helmet and tried to repeat what she'd done in the cave. She focused until her face strained.

Nothing.

Greg peeled off the floor, led by his broad chest. Phlip sat paralyzed in the corner opposite the scene, frozen so perfectly he looked carved.

Jerro was pushing to his feet when the blood-red light extinguished in an instant.

A series of precise blue orbs zipped through the room, striking the cloaked figures one after another. The impact snapped them backward into the emptied shelves.

Greg dropped hard to the floor, rolled with a groan, and clutched his head.

The lamp flared back to life.

Around the corner, the hearth fire returned, ripping into full, flickering brightness, without a moment's weakness.

In the doorway stood an old mole-rat, wrapped in tattered brown robes. His wrinkled, hairless skin formed smooth flats and deep creases. A grid of tattoos rose from beneath the robe collar. A thick beaded necklace hung on his narrow frame. Several long silver hairs were woven into thin eyebrows above stormy, clouded eyes.

A single blue diamond faded from his forehead, the apex of a triangle formed by his eyes and the mark. Its glow was light blue, then gone.

Mari's paws fell to her sides. Her eyes widened like she needed more space for what she was seeing.

"Rufus?"

"Yes," Rufus said, voice calm and weirdly cheerful. "Gather your friends and hurry. We're already behind time."

He snapped his head hard right and shouted down the hall, "Batten down the hatches, ye scallywags!"

Mari blinked, still catching up. "Rufus, what's going on? Who are they?"

"No one you can reason with," Rufus said, and vanished to the right where the hallway ended in a bookshelf.

Mari helped Jerro up. Jerro reached for Greg and hauled him to his feet. Phlip remained in the corner, a pile of pellets at his feet.

"And grab that map on my desk while you're at it," Rufus called, sounding farther away than he should have been.

"Of course it's a map," Mari said.

Jerro shrugged and retracted the parchment into its case, tucking it into his bomber jacket. "Guess so. That actually makes a lot of sense."

Greg sagged, slow to move. Jerro came back, pulled Greg's arm over his shoulder, and guided him toward the hall. Greg groaned and went pale, the green tint creeping in.

"Hang on," Greg muttered. He reeled and heaved up a pile of thick, chunky white slime onto the floor.

"I'm sorry, Rufus," Greg slurred, wiping the corner of his mouth with a paw. "I'll clean it up."

"Lemme get ten coins and a ticket to the cinema, see!" Rufus echoed from down the hall in an odd nasal voice.

Mari stepped into the hall, then froze. She poked her head around the corner, listened, and dragged back.

"Guys," she said quietly, "let's go. Come on."

The bookshelf in the hall had swung open, revealing stone steps leading down into a lined corridor. Candles appeared every so often, lighting the way in warm, wavering pockets.

They descended, following Rufus's voice as it drifted ahead.

As they neared the end of the hall, they heard him again. "Sector nineteen has been lost. The galactic fleet is scattered between systems. Our forces are in—" He halted.

The corridor opened into a round chamber with a low ceiling. The gray floor segmented into slices that joined at a point in the center.

Rufus hovered on the far side, legs crossed, paws resting in his lap. His fingers formed a circle, index and thumb touching like he held an invisible ball.

"Ah, wonderful," Rufus said. "I'm glad you all could join me this fine evening. We have little time."

"Yeah," Mari said. "You mentioned that already."

"Oh, did I?" Rufus replied brightly. "Apologies."

Jerro stepped forward. "Rufus, what were those creatures?"

Rufus's eyes rolled back. His paws extended, palms down. His fingers drifted from side to side like he was playing invisible keys. Then his eyes snapped forward, and he froze, staring at the trio.

"I must speak quickly," he said, voice flattening. "I don't know how much longer I have. There has been a fissure in the fabric of time. The three of you are critical in repairing the damage. The events of the last lune are connected and will be explained in time, but for now I need you to trust—"

He stopped mid-thought.

Mari, Greg, and Jerro looked at each other, then back to him. The silence stretched just long enough to feel dangerous.

Rufus's eyes rolled back again. He dropped his legs to the floor and began fencing an invisible opponent with grace and speed that didn't match his frame.

"En garde!" he shouted.

A dash forward. A quick riposte. A flurry to finish. He bowed and pulled a nonexistent mask from his face.

Mari's stomach turned. Greg's brow tightened, calculating. Jerro didn't blink, as if he was afraid the room would change again if he did.

Rufus paused.

Slowly turned back to them.

Then he picked up where he'd left off, like nothing had happened.

"This is a transit station," he said, drifting toward the center of the chamber and opening his arms. "With the proper key, it will take us to a pocket of isolated time where this malady cannot reach my mind, and we can assess the next steps." His tone tightened. "Quickly now. We have only moments."

Mari stepped forward, then hesitated. "Wait. We'll be able to come back, right? My father needs me."

"It can't be certain," Rufus said. A sly smile slid into place. "However, by taking this step, you open a door to reunite with..." He paused, choosing carefully. "Others you thought to be lost."

Soft footsteps hustled in the connecting hallway above.

Greg's eyes flicked to the ceiling, then to Mari. "He's losing himself," he said out of the corner of his mouth. "But those cloaked things are coming, and I don't like what they can do."

Jerro swallowed, jaw tight. "Deepworks wasn't a story," he said. "If Rufus is our only dig out, then we take it."

Mari's gaze darted toward the hall, then down to Phlip. Her paw found his harness and closed around it like a promise. "Together," she said, more to herself than to them.

Greg nodded once, firm. Jerro answered with the smallest tilt of his head.

They moved.

The three friends and Phlip ran onto the segmented platform.

Mari looked past Rufus toward the hall as a small contingent of cloaked figures breached the chamber. She began to lift, feet rolling from heel to toe, the ground letting go of her in slow increments.

The creatures unleashed fierce screeches. Their blasts were swept upward and vanished through the ceiling.

A muffled roar replaced the repulsive screams.

The world sundered.

Everything dissolved as a rush of energy pulsed through their bodies. Tingling radiated from their core through the tips of their paws.

A final sound echoed dully in their ears, like a distant explosion heard through stone.

For a brief second, before the shattered image of the short gray room fully vanished, Mari saw it again in the streaming energy.

That face from the cave.

She had thought it was her mother, but this time it took on an ambiguous form, shifting at the edges. The visage swirled in residual particulate and disappeared as the only world they had ever known faded from existence.

CHAPTER 7 | STATION

A chromatic waterfall swallowed their vision. Their feet lifted, then landed on something cold and smooth. The stretched world snapped back into focus as the colors remembered their shapes. Spicy cucumber, with a hint of mint, flashed across their tongues.

They stood on a dark gray circular platform with an inward-sloped rim, its surface divided into thin triangular slices that met at a single point. The same segmented pad from Rufus's basement, but everything around it had changed.

Above, they couldn't tell if they were looking at a ceiling or a sky. A star-salted void hung overhead, too bright, too close. Streams of color streaked through it. Every so often something shimmered, and the truth revealed itself. An iridescent dome, catching the backdrop and bending it out of true.

Sound arrived late. At first, it was a discordant rush, then it sorted itself, note by note, like a symphony warming into coherence. Pressure built between their ears, then popped like a balloon.

Rufus's voice cut through first. "Welcome to Station."

Mari, Jerro, and Greg stared at each other. Phlip dropped a quick pile of pellets and scratched one floppy ear like this was all perfectly normal.

A walkway extended from the platform, straight as a dock.

Mari followed the line of it, and her stomach tightened. There was no water underneath. No floor. Just a slow churn of space, like an ocean made of dark ether. The dock and the facility beyond it hovered over nothing, as if gravity had been politely asked not to interfere.

Rufus rotated toward the walkway and drifted forward, levitating with casual ease. "Follow me. I'll give you a quick tour as we make our way to your quarters."

"What is this place?" Mari asked. "And what did you mean about seeing someone we lost?"

"This is Station," Rufus said, not slowing. "Removed from the fabric of space and time. Where we are is… abstract."

They tried to follow, but their legs argued.

Jerro stumbled and hit the walkway. Mari managed three steps before she dropped to a knee, muscles quaking like her strength had been left behind in The Burrow.

Rufus chuckled ahead of them. "First transit malaise. Typical. Keep moving."

Greg hauled Jerro up and made small circles on Mari's back. "Come on. He's getting ahead of us."

They pushed forward, and that was when the ships came into view.

Row after row lined the dock in tight berths. Some were sleek gunmetal wedges with subtle illumination. Others looked stitched together from scavenged panels and strange materials that caught the rainbow light and threw it back in unfamiliar colors. None of them floated. They hovered, steady over the abyss.

Crews loaded and unloaded cargo with practiced speed. Some were burrowing rodents like them. Others were not. Tall, hunched, armored. A sailor paused, saw Rufus, and saluted.

Rufus kept talking like it meant nothing. "Back in the day, we had to climb into the godunum of cows and other ungulates capable of bridging the space-time continuum. Not the most pleasant way to travel."

"Guys," Mari muttered, "he's out of his mind."

"Might be," Greg said, "but so were those cloaked things back there."

They passed a smaller ship, and a marmot sailor hopped down, tapped the hull once, and the whole craft collapsed into a ball. He tossed it to another sailor—a lumbering badger—and jogged off.

Jerro slowed, staring. "Did you just see that—"

Before he could finish, a caravan of capybaras expanded something wagon-shaped into a full ship in an empty berth. Boards unfolded. Panels locked into place in a smooth mechanical cascade. They climbed aboard without breaking stride.

Mari's eyes kept drifting outward, beyond the dock, beyond the facility. Outside the dome, a sphere of blue energy slid past, trailing a glinting silver wake. Farther out, two pink bubbles spread from a band of light. On the opposite side, a ring of dark clouds produced beams so bright they seemed to carve the darkness itself.

Nothing about the motion felt stable. Not wrong. Just untrustworthy. Like her senses were reading from a different set of rules.

Ahead, sleek towers clustered within three massive rings, dragging through space vertically, so tall Mari couldn't see their full curve at once.

"What are those?" she asked before she meant to.

Rufus glanced back, eyes bright. "You'll learn, but not now."

Then, near the end of the dock, an armored guard in deep red garnet plating waited at attention. Two curved swords hung at her waist, one shorter than the other.

Rufus addressed her with the ease of routine. "Master Larude. Always a pleasure. These three are the newest recruits. Mari, Jerro, and Greg." He paused, then winked at Phlip. "Oh, and Phlip too."

Phlip's glassy eyes drifted into the void.

Master Larude drew the short sword with lightning speed, flourished it in a display so precise Mari couldn't follow the blade, and finished by presenting it vertically. With a flick of her head, she raised her visor.

"Welcome to Station, young Fragments," she said, voice flat and serious. "May your journeys be nonlinear."

"Thanks… I think?" Mari answered, her tone rising and falling like a question she didn't mean to ask.

"Come along, come along," Rufus said, already drifting past her. "We've much to do, much to do indeed."

They followed, leaving Master Larude at her post.

"What do you think she meant by that?" Greg murmured, "and what even was she?"

"Oh," Jerro said, lighting with recognition. "I think I know. I was reading about them the other day in a pre-war book. She's a wombut, maybe? If I'm right, they live in a different part of the world. Far from The Burrow." He frowned. "No idea about the nonlinear journey part, though."

"Very close, Jerro," Rufus called back, and they all looked up, startled he'd overheard them at that distance. "Master Larude is a wombat. Prime Spectre of Astral Landing. The landing includes the pathway we just walked, and the chronoarch we just used to travel here. The nonlinear journey phrase is used by the Eternal Spectre Guard."

Greg threw his arms up and turned about like a carousel. "I really don't understand any of this. Where are we even?"

"Imagine, if you will," Rufus said, "your universe is a finely woven tapestry. The multiverse is an infinite stack of tapestry layers. They touch, but do not intertwine. This place is a thread that runs through those layers."

Greg's eyes expanded. He tucked in his chin and flattened his lips. "Yeah. Totally makes sense." He nodded vigorously while shooting Jerro and Mari a look that clearly meant the opposite.

Jerro grinned. "I think I get it."

Mari said nothing. She walked beside Phlip, a paw resting on his harness, eyes fixed on the ground, holding on like she could keep herself real that way.

Ahead, an open-air cantina came into view, bright and busy compared to the stark gray structures that pressed around it. Creatures moved in and out in a constant flow. Burrowing rodents, beavers, capybaras, porcupines, and others Mari couldn't name.

Mari looked up as they drew closer. "Rufus, why did she call us Fragments?"

"Because you are," Rufus said. "By rank and by reality. When we used the chronoarch, the timeline fragmented. That's how new initiates begin. As Fragments. You are still you, but not wholly the same you."

"I don't feel fragmented," Greg said.

"And you wouldn't," Rufus replied. "Your mind cannot hold the full shape of it. Not yet."

Greg nodded again, exaggerated and empty. "Oh. Okay. And the rank part?"

"We keep structure for function, not discipline," Rufus said. "Fragments. Then Weavers. Then Elision."

Jerro glanced toward the cantina crowd. "So what are they? Everyone here?"

"Everyone on Station is Unbound," Rufus said. "Freelance crews. Travelers. Staff."

Greg pointed at himself with a jerk of his chin. "So we're Unbound too?"

Rufus's smile twitched. "Yes, but you are also initiates now. You belong to the Order. So long as you chose to. Your rank for the moment is Fragment."

Jerro's brow furrowed. "So we are in the Eternal Spectres?"

"The Eternal Spectre Guard. They are sentinels for Station," Rufus said. "They are not you. You are something else."

Mari sped up to walk beside him. "You said the timeline was ruptured, but now you're saying it fragmented. Did we do that?"

"Fragmentation is normal," Rufus said. "Every decision, every step, every breath can branch. Rupturing is different. Destructive. Picture that stack of tapestries moving through time. Each fragment creates a copy of the stack. Those copies diverge and evolve. When there is a rupture, the stack collapses on itself. Layers can meld, not only within a stack, but the failure can propagate between stacks."

Mari's brow tightened. "So where do we come in?"

"That," Rufus said, "is to be determined." His cheeks lifted into a smile that somehow made Mari want to believe him. "Truthfully, it is an art more than a science. Each artist finds their own medium." His eyes flicked to hers. "I know you will find your way. Just as your mother did."

"Wait," Mari said. "My mother?"

But Rufus had already turned toward the group, cutting her off.

"Alright. Here is where I leave you for the time being." He waved a paw at the cantina. "This is The Hub. Gathering place for all of Station."

He gestured toward a table, directing them to sit. Mari stayed on his flank, unwilling to let the mention of her mother evaporate.

Rufus gestured again, this time with his eyes and head added to the motion. "Grellin and Mellin will take care of you. Get the three of you set up in your room. We will continue orientation when you awake for the new lune."

"Who?" Mari asked, looking around.

Rufus vanished.

Two gerbils popped their heads up over the edge of the table like they'd been hiding there the whole time.

"Greetings, young Fragments!" they beamed in unison.

"I'm Grellin," said the tan one with a white belly.

The other was black with white blotches. She leaned in front of Grellin. "And I'm Mellin." Her words hung in the middle.

"First things first," Grellin said, "how about we get a round of ice cream for this gang? You all look plain ol' tuckered out."

Mellin elbowed him. "Look at their wrists. They don't have trackers," she said, quieter than Grellin but not quiet enough.

"By the Trimarmot, you're right!" Grellin said, not subtly at all. "Hang on. I'll be right back." He scurried off toward the bar.

Mellin turned back to them, tone gentler. "Don't worry, this isn't completely uncommon, but I have to ask. When did you last have ice cream?"

Jerro blinked. "Uh… never?" He looked to Greg and Mari like he needed confirmation.

"Never?" Mellin's head cocked back. "Well, you all are in for a treat." Her eyes narrowed with sudden seriousness. "But it's very important to remember you cannot have more than twenty-seven ounces in a seventy-three-lune period. But, if you have just the right amount, you will experience certain… benefits." Then she smiled again. "Plus, it's simply delicious."

Jerro stared. "Is that a Burrow lune? How are you measuring time here?"

"Most of us are originally from The Burrow," Mellin said with a shrug, "or variations at least. Since time is… flexible here, we stuck with the traditional lune."

Grellin returned, trailed by a levitating tray with three ice cream cones holstered to it. Glossy white scoops embedded with black flecks reflected the rainbow glow outside. Waffle cones waited beneath, crisp and brown.

Cradled in Grellin's paws was a stack of three matte black bands, so tall it nearly overshadowed him.

"Alright," Grellin said, breathless with excitement. "These trackers are multifunctional. They ping your location in space and time back to Station, track ice cream intake, and monitor eldritch radiation. Slap one on and you're good."

"The one thing they won't do is tell you the time," Mellin added brightly, "but you'll find that isn't super relevant in most cases."

The friends stared blankly.

"Hold your wrists out," Mellin said. "I'll show you."

Greg went first. Then Jerro. Then Mari, slower than the others, her eyes still trying to make sense of the world outside the dome. Mellin held a bracelet just above each wrist, then smacked it down. The rigid band flexed and wrapped perfectly. Not too tight. Not too loose.

"If you ever need to take it off," Grellin said, "just grab an end and straighten it back out like this." He demonstrated, popping his own band free, straightening it, then snapping it back around his tiny wrist.

With their bracelets on, they tried ice cream for the first time.

Hesitant at first. Then the first bite hit, cold enough to sting and sweet enough to make them blink, vanilla hiding underneath. The scoops softened fast, turning it into a countdown. They ate quicker than planned, catching drips before they could fall, paws growing tacky as the cone warmed and slumped. Somehow it held together to the end, the last crunch snapping clean between their teeth.

Their bracelets buzzed in near unison. On each matte band, a small ice cream cone icon blinked to life and filled partway from the bottom up.

Grellin and Mellin watched with bright, proud smiles, but didn't eat any themselves.

Mari pushed the final bit of cone into her mouth, cheeks puffing. "How come you're not having any?"

They held up their wrists.

"We're tapped out on our dose," Grellin said. Mellin double-tapped her bracelet, and a hollow ice cream cone icon appeared on the matte surface, filled from the bottom up, then flashed rapidly.

"What did you think?" Grellin asked, leaning in. "How was it?"

"That was insane," Mari said, swallowing. "So good." Her brow tightened again. "But what benefits are you talking about?"

Mellin grinned and folded her arms. "Let's just say you'll notice your powers run significantly stronger in the coming lunes."

Grellin clapped his paws once. "Okay. We gotta get you all to your room. Rufus told us not to let you linger here too long."

Greg looked at his friends. "When did he tell them that?"

Mellin and Grellin were already moving toward the edge of The Hub. "Follow us!"

Mari stood, still half stunned. "I don't know, but I'm only following like ten percent of what's going on right now."

"That's weird," Jerro said, holding back a smile with flat lips and wide eyes. "I'm understanding exactly forty-three percent of it."

They followed the gerbils out.

The Hub was bright and expansive, its walls covered in action-packed murals of alien landscapes and unfamiliar creatures. Dozens of tables filled the space. A long ice cream bar curved in a half-circle, stools lining its edge. Behind the bar, displays cycled through images of crystals of various colors and sizes being grown in a strange digital setting.

Outside between buildings, the air felt thinner, colder, and somehow cleaner.

They didn't walk far before Mellin let out a small squeak and announced, "This is it. Home sweet home!"

"When you wake up, swing back to The Hub," Grellin said in a sweet yet firm tone. "We'll help you get going with the rest of your orientation. Get some rest, ya little Fragments."

Greg opened the door.

They all muttered goodbyes to Grellin and Mellin, then stepped into their new quarters and let the day collapse behind them.

CHAPTER 8 | TRANSIT

Mari, Jerro, Greg, and Phlip stepped into their new quarters.

From the outside, it looked like nothing more than a modest apartment tucked among others. But when Greg eased the door open, a rich aroma rolled out to meet them. Roasted vegetables. Freshly dug earth. Warm stone after rain.

Inside, the walls were lined with dirt, bioluminescent fungi, and root work, so familiar it made Mari's chest loosen. Like The Burrow had reached out and recreated itself here. In the back corner, a small waterfall spilled into a pond held by a short dam. The water should have eaten up half the living space, but somehow the room stretched wider than any apartment had a right to.

Calm washed over them. The disorientation of Station didn't fade, exactly. It was more like the room made space for it, letting the discomfort bleed out in slow, quiet breaths.

The cozy dwelling was loosely divided into an entryway and a common room. On the left of the entryway sat a straw-bedded stall sized for a riding rabbit, stocked with hay, carrots, and water. On the right, tall, sleek equipment lockers stood beside a small ready space — clean and orderly, like it expected a team to move through fast.

Beyond that, the common room opened wide. A large table waited at its center, heaped with food. Perfectly roasted honey-glazed carrots. Butter potatoes. Crisp sliced beets. Mixed nuts that smelled toasted and sweet.

A compact kitchen filled one corner. The other held cozy seating: three high-backed lounge chairs and a wooden slab coffee table set between them. Two circular doorways opened off the side walls, one smaller, one larger.

Greg turned in a slow circle, eyes narrowed like he was trying to catch the seams in the illusion. "Was this made for us?"

Yes.

The voice wasn't from the kitchen. Or the waterfall. Or the hallway.

It just… existed in mindspace, gentle and matter-of-fact.

The three friends stared at each other.

"Did you hear that?" Mari whispered.

They all nodded.

Phlip did not. He had already flopped onto the straw, a carrot propped between his paws. He took quick bites from the end as if this was exactly the correct response to interdimensional relocation.

The voice returned, still soft, still calm.

I'm Lunda. A Series-Seven inorganic intelligence developed by Marmatech. The moment you arrived on Station, I scanned your neural networks and cross-referenced them against Station's collective knowledge to generate an ideal living space based on your needs and desires. Please make yourselves comfortable. If there is anything you need, you don't have to say anything. I will already know.

Mari blinked hard. "Okay. I have so many questions."

"Same," Jerro said, and there was no humor in it. "I don't love the part where you scanned us without asking."

Greg swung his head toward Jerro. "What? Come on. Beavers are masters at this stuff. Isn't this your thing?"

"Beavers use a *modified* form of telepathy," Jerro said, irritation twitching his ears. "We can influence behavior, sometimes implant a suggestion if the mind is open to it. But this?" He gestured vaguely at the air like he wanted to grab the concept and shake it. "This isn't feeling and intuition. This is data. Full access. It's a pure form of telepathy unlike anything I've ever come across."

While they argued, Mari slipped between them, marched to one of the lounge chairs, and tossed her bag beside it. She plopped onto the cushion and pulled a small pillow into her lap as though she were claiming territory.

"Lunda," Mari said, forcing her voice steady. "What are Unbound? Rufus said something similar, you mean us right?"

Yes. You are Unbound. You are no longer tied to a single thread of the tapestry, to use Rufus's analogy. You are free to move across tapestries, unbound by the laws of space-time.

Jerro sat in the chair beside her, posture rigid. "Why are we Unbound?"

Lunda's presence didn't shift, but the mental layer felt cleaner when she answered. Like the question got filed, indexed, and returned.

The logic of why is not found in my database. Any intelligence can become Unbound. Organic minds often struggle to ground themselves after severance. The three of you demonstrate unusually high resiliency. That in turn increases recursive stability.

Mari's eyes darted between Jerro and Greg. "What if we don't want this? Don't want to be here. What if we just go back to The Burrow, back to our families?"

There was a pause. Not hesitation. Calculation.

If you could return now, The Burrow you know will cease to exist. As will Station. As will everything.

Silence settled like dust.

"But we *can* go back someday," Mari said, and it wasn't a question. She made it a statement because she needed it to be one.

There are possible futures where you return to The Burrow.

The answer landed heavier than Mari expected. She felt it in the way Jerro stopped blinking—in the way Greg's jaw tightened around nothing.

"What about our families?" Mari asked, voice thinning. "Our lives. What will they even think happened to us?"

That depends on what happens to you. You are no longer experiencing time within a linear referential framework. In theory, time in your tapestry and time for you are severed. You may return as if nothing occurred. You may return after your bodies have aged. You may never return.

Greg stood abruptly and stalked to the table. He grabbed a pawful of nuts and started feeding them through his incisors one by one, like crunching something small could keep him from thinking about something enormous.

"I don't get any of this," he said around a bite, "and I don't even care anymore." He crunched another nut. "My dad would've made my life miserable back home."

Mari's eyes sharpened. Her lips pressed into one corner, then she forced herself to look away. Back to Jerro. Back to the chairs. Back to something that wasn't Greg's voice, pretending it wasn't cracked.

"Can't you see the future?" Mari asked Lunda. "You said you have knowledge of these different times, tapestries or whatever. Does that not include us?"

There is no future without a linear referential framework. There is only the present. There is only what is happening and what is not.

Mari stared into the room like she could find the edge of that statement and peel it back.

Jerro's tail flopped off the side of his chair as he shifted, restless. "Lunda. The things I encountered in Deepworks. What were they?"

Hyrax. Organics of unspecified origin. Database records suggest their first appearance in several alternate tapestries related to yours. Markers in their base code indicate engineered biology, accompanied by an anomalous sequence of nucleotides in their DNA structure.

"Hyrax," Jerro repeated softly, like naming it could pin it down.

Mari dug through her bag and pulled out the rubbing from the cave, holding it up even though she suspected Lunda didn't need eyes.

"Lunda, what do you know about this? Can you see it?"

Scanning database… I have no record of this symbol or associated writing. The script aligns with markers from a dated language in your home tapestry.

"What language?" Mari asked instantly.

The language derives from a short-lived intelligent organic species that existed on your home world. Variations of their record span approximately three million solar cycles. The final record of their presence is over five hundred solar cycles prior to your perceived time.

Jerro leaned forward. "What happened to them?"

They were equipped with more intelligence than wisdom. Their tribal nature resulted in intensive wars that ravaged the atmosphere and led to their end. Your recorded history refers to them as the Ancients.

An image formed in their minds.

Hairless. Upright. Two long lower limbs. Feet flattened, toes splayed. Arms outstretched, finger to finger as long as it was tall. Shaggy hair crested the head and rolled down the sides.

This is a reconstruction—

Mari shot to her feet so fast the pillow hit the floor.

"I've seen this," she said, breath sharp. "Or... I dreamed it."

Jerro turned toward her. "What was the dream?"

Greg returned from the nuts, brows lifted. "What dream? Was it like the cave?"

Mari told them. The floating. The warm, dense liquid. The apparatus over her mouth that let her breathe. The hairless paw that wasn't hers. The long fingers. Her mind raced back to the cave.

Jerro and Greg exchanged a look that said, too many coincidences and none of them are safe.

"This has to be connected," Jerro said. "Rufus, Station, all of it. It's too strange not to be."

Greg nodded, slow and firm.

"And when I woke up in the cave," Mari added, "there was a figure carved above the doorway. One of the Ancients. But it was shown with burrowing rodents, standing alongside them. Like a friend." She swallowed. "What do you know about that, Lunda?"

Lunda's presence felt steady, but the answer carried a faint edge of limitation.

There is no recorded overlap in your tapestry. However, as I explained, time being nonlinear makes the database unreliable. Imagine trying to assemble a puzzle using only its shadow. In a mirror. While an interloper rearranges the pieces. I can identify shapes. Sometimes connect them accurately in the moment. But the scene is fleeting.

Jerro slumped back and rested his head on one paw, elbow braced on the armrest. He stared at the loaded table without really seeing it.

Then he spoke without lifting his head, voice warped by his palm. "We should eat and get some rest. Tomorrow we keep piecing it together." He paused, then deepened his voice dramatically and sat upright to deliver it properly. "My grandpa always says, 'you shouldn't build a dam when you're tired or hungry.'"

Mari snorted unexpectedly.

Greg leaned on the tall backrest of his chair, shoulders and head poking over the top. He flexed his thick chest muscles to bounce himself against the upholstery like the chair owed him answers.

"I don't even know what we're supposed to be doing tomorrow."

"You're right," Mari said, exhaustion suddenly settling into her bones. "I have no idea what's going on. But I can't think anymore."

She stood, grabbed her bag, and pointed at the smaller circular doorway. "I'm assuming this is my room?"

Yes.

"Perfect. See you guys later." She snagged a glazed carrot off the table as she walked and vanished through the smaller door without waiting for any reply.

Greg watched her go, then exhaled like a slow deflation. "Guess I'll hit the dirt as well."

Jerro nodded, then he and Greg automatically fell into their routine. It started simple. Crossing high fives that worked from high to low. Then the rotational tail slap. Then foot-paw bumps as they hopped from leg to leg.

Jerro usually struggled with the hop part.

He nailed it this time.

They finished with a paw clasp and pulled each other in for a quick one-arm hug and a chest bump.

When it was done, Jerro scurried toward the pond and dam. "Night, buddy."

Greg had already ducked into the larger side doorway, then popped his head back out. "See you in a blink!"

Mari didn't answer. She was already gone.

Their rooms were perfectly appointed, each in its own quiet way. Not too large, not too small.

Mari's bed was soft. Her room held a desk with art supplies and gear for exploring.

Greg's bed was firm. His room had a sparring dummy in the corner.

Jerro's bed was slightly damp. His room held a workbench with tools and equipment arranged with unsettling care, every item waiting in the spot he would have chosen.

Phlip didn't care about any of that. He was already splooted across his straw bed, ears flopped over his face, snoring like nothing in the multiverse had ever been simpler.

The quarters went quiet. Water fell in a steady hush. Phlip's snores filled the gaps.

In her room, Mari stared into the warm darkness, backlit by a small orb of contained fireflies flickering softly in the corner.

∞

Sleep took her gently.

She was back in the cave.

The mural stretched across the stone wall, unchanged. Ancient symbols glowed faintly within the rock, breathing in slow pulses. The language still hovered just beyond understanding, familiar and un-reachable.

Then, the symbols began to move.

Letters loosened from the stone and slid across its surface. Shapes rotated, nested, unfolded. The mural rearranged itself with quiet intention, forming words she could finally read.

THE BURROWING RODENT EMPIRE EXISTS WITHIN

THIS VESSEL CARRIES ON

AN ETERNAL DIG

A BURROW WITH NO END

The words held steady, glowing brighter than the rest.

∞

It is time to awaken.

Lunda's voice brushed Mari's mind.

Mari jolted upright, heart racing.

Hadn't we just fallen asleep? She thought, the question already dissolving as the memory slipped away.

She slid out of bed and crossed to her desk in two quick steps. She grabbed paper and scribbled the words down before they could fade, paw cramping with urgency. Then she tugged on her vest, folded the note, and tucked it into a pocket.

When she stepped back into the common room, the smell hit her first.

Breakfast.

Fruits. Nutty pancakes. Warm syrup.

Jerro and Greg stumbled out of their rooms a moment later, blinking as if the light was too loud. Phlip waddled up to Mari's chair and pressed his giant head against her side with a quiet, needy huff.

Mari piled pancakes onto her plate and didn't stop until the stack leaned. Syrup. Fruit. More syrup. She cut wedges and shoveled them in like her body was trying to out-eat her brain.

Before she'd even cleared her mouth, she started talking.

"Guys," she said thickly, "I had more of that dream."

Jerro looked up, already curious. He was slicing one pancake into perfect portions, placing one berry on each bite like it mattered. "What happened?"

Mari pulled out her note, unfolded it, and read it to them. She explained fast, like speed could keep it real.

"The Burrowing Rodent… Empire?" Greg repeated. "That's what it said?"

"Yeah." Mari swallowed. "That's what it said."

Greg's brow furrowed. "I think I remember reading something about that in one of Rufus's books when we were younger. I thought it was just a story. It was written like fiction."

"Sometimes the truest stories are the ones we don't expect," Rufus said from the front doorway.

All three of them snapped their heads around at once.

"Rufus!" they said in unison.

Jerro stood halfway. "You've got to tell us more. What is happening? Why is Mari having these dreams?"

"All things in time," Rufus said, calm as ever. "All things in time."

Mari leaned forward, words tripping over each other. "Can you at least tell me *why* I don't remember going to that cave?"

"Cave?" Rufus repeated.

"Yeah. Before last lune. I woke up in this cave and was going to come see if you knew what was going on, but then the hylux—" Mari stopped herself, and her eyes flicked to Jerro.

"Hyrax," Rufus corrected automatically. His expression stayed composed, but his gaze slid past them, unfocused, attention snagged on something not present in the room.

Mari started to explain the dream again, but Rufus lifted one paw, cutting through it.

"Come along," he said. "We have much to do before you set off on your first mission."

Jerro mouthed the question they were all thinking.

Mission?

Rufus turned and walked out. The three friends looked at each other, confusion now so familiar it almost felt like routine, and followed.

They passed The Hub, busy now with all sorts of creatures. A swarm of rats ran by, chatting in a foreign language that shifted in Mari's mind until it became comprehensible. Moles ate breakfast at a smaller table. Nearby, a group of wombats in garnet armor sat with their helmets off, sipping something that smelled of mint and earth.

At the curved ice cream bar, Grellin and Mellin spotted the group as they passed. They waved, pointed at their bracelets, and Mellin presented an ice cream cone. Just large enough for them to make out at that distance.

A raccoon hurried past and bumped into one of the armored figures, sending a splash of tea airborne.

In one swift motion, the wombat shot out a leg to steady the raccoon, set the cup down, and slid the saucer to catch the errant tea before it touched the table.

The raccoon apologized profusely, bowing and backing away until it bumped into another table. A long-snouted creature lowered a hose-like nose into a bowl. The contents undulated and separated into individual units.

Ants.

Mari took a step away so fast her stomach lurched.

"First things first," Rufus said, resuming his effortless hovering so their pace had to quicken. "We need to get you to the outfitter. Set up your accounts. Get you any necessary gear. Then we head to the chief navigator and see what ships are available."

The crowd parted instinctively as they moved through. Some stopped and whispered. Others stared. Most simply carried on like this was normal, like new Fragments being hustled along by Rufus was a common morning event.

They approached a prominent building, a stacked cylinder of polished ivory stone that caught the chromatic sky and threw it back in a soft sheen. Each layer hovered, inset above the next. Golden light glowed from the gaps. A deep trill reverberated between the stratified sections as they neared.

Steps led down into the entrance, sunk below floor level.

The sign above it blazed MARMATECH, bold and backlit.

Inside, marmots in green-and-white striped uniforms moved with practiced efficiency. A young marmot spotted Rufus and sprinted over to salute.

Rufus returned it. "Get these three set up with an account and the standard mission provision load out."

"Yes, sir!" the marmot chirped.

Rufus turned to the group. "I have things to attend to. I'll return shortly and take you to the landing."

Then he vanished without a sound, as though the air simply decided it no longer needed him.

The young marmot pivoted back to them. "Alright. Follow me. Name's Ferdi. I'm gonna help you new Fragments get set so you don't die your first time out of the chromosphere."

They all stopped.

Greg spoke first, voice flat with disbelief. "Excuse me. Did you just say—*die*?"

Ferdi didn't flinch. "Yeah. Eight out of every ten Fragments die on their first solo transit." He finally noticed Greg's expression and hurried to patch it. "But… I'm sure you guys will do great! I can see it in your—" He looked them up and down, grasping for the word. "Fur! The way the void filaments refract psionic energy. You've got latent power. *Big* stuff."

Greg looked at Mari and Jerro with a furrowed brow.

Jerro shrugged.

Mari just stared at Ferdi like she was trying to decide whether panic belonged on the schedule today.

Ferdi launched into motion, pulling up a series of holo displays. Jerro leaned in instantly, eyes tracking how the interface assembled itself.

"First things first," Ferdi said, pointing. "Hold your wristbands up to the scanner."

They did, one by one. Mari first. Greg second. Jerro third.

On Jerro's scan, the device chirped and stuttered.

Ferdi frowned. "Hmm. Let me see that." He popped Jerro's band off, straightened it with a click, then slapped it back on. "Try again. Sometimes they get buggy, and you just have to re-slap them."

Jerro tried again. This time it beeped clean.

Ferdi nodded as if he'd expected nothing else. "Perfect. Now. Loadouts."

He guided them toward a section of the store and grabbed backpacks.

Mari lifted hers slightly. "I already have a bag."

"You sure do," Ferdi said, cheerful. "Mind if I take a look?"

Before Mari could answer, he was inspecting it. He reached inside, made a few quick adjustments, and a mechanical whirring came from somewhere in the pack's guts.

"Okay," Ferdi said, delighted. "Check this out. Dimensional pocket storage."

He grabbed a long wooden stick from a nearby aisle and slid it into Mari's bag. The bag should not have been able to hold it.

The stick vanished inside like it had never existed.

Jerro stepped closer, prodding the pack with a paw, fascinated. "You are *absolutely* going to have to show me how this works."

"Anytime!" Ferdi said. "Our beaver engineers are the best in the multiverse. They'd love a fresh mind to mold." He pointed at Jerro and grabbed another wooden stick. "This one's for you, by the way. Classic beaver stick. You know what to do with it."

Jerro stared at the stick.

He did not, in fact, know what to do with it.

He nodded anyway.

Greg nodded too, because the nod had become a survival tactic.

It turned out Ferdi also did not know what to do with it, but nobody said anything, so it counted as knowledge.

Ferdi started chucking supplies into their bags with reckless confidence.

"Standard rations," he said. "Pizza is a staple. Also, biscuits, beloved." Boxes disappeared into the dimensional pockets one after another.

"Water," Ferdi continued, glancing at Mari and Greg. "We know you can store up to fifty times your bodyweight by compressing it in your interstitial void space."

Mari froze mid-blink. Greg froze mid-chew.

Ferdi turned to Jerro. "But you, sir beaver, cannot. So." He produced a pitcher like he was presenting a trophy. "Micro portal to the dimension of Aquarius. It pours continuously. I've seen a small lake form once when one got knocked over and forgotten about, so… don't do that." He laughed as though it were a fun story.

Jerro stared at the pitcher with cautious horror.

"Vectorization rakes," Ferdi said, tossing long blue tools into their kits. "Automated degaussers. And the latest XB-series field-portable hyperbaric chamber." His eyes tracked the list in his head, counting off what remained. "That should do it for psionic first aid and recovery items."

He paused, fingers hovering over the holo display. "We don't charge Fragments, but we track your gear so we can build custom kits later, assuming you survi—" He coughed. "Survey the multiverse."

Mari opened her mouth to respond, but Rufus materialized behind Ferdi so silently Mari felt her fur rise before her mind even caught up.

Ferdi saw their faces shift.

He tried to look back without turning his head. Only his eyes moved. "Master Rufus is behind me, isn't he?"

The three friends nodded.

Ferdi spun and saluted. "All finished, sir!"

Rufus smiled and drifted around the young marmot. "Thank you, Ferdi. We have one more stop before you go."

They exited Marmatech. Outside, Phlip had fallen asleep in the open, trusting the world more than he should have. Mari whistled softly, and he bounded up, ears flopping, then trotted after them, paws drumming lightly on the metal surface.

"Rufus," Mari said immediately, trying to grab the thread before it slipped away again, "where are we going? What is going on? You've—"

Rufus stopped and turned toward them. He stepped closer, gaze settling on Mari first, then widening to include all three.

"Mari," he said, voice steady, "I'm not trying to be cryptic. There are simply things that cannot be explained. Things unknown but felt." His eyes softened. "What I can say is this. The three of you, and Phlip of course, have an unpredictable but critical role to play in correcting the rupture."

Mari's eyes glazed with helpless frustration. "Rufus... I just want to go home."

Rufus looked her up and down like he was seeing more than her fur and her posture.

Then his smile warmed.

"Mari," he said, "you are home."

He pulled Jerro and Greg in with one arm, stacking them shoulder to shoulder in a loose arc. "Wherever the three of you go. Together. That is home. Your strength comes from your bond. That's the best advice I can give you."

They approached a skinny tower now, with a circular disk forming its head. Heavy metal doors slid open as they neared, disappearing into the sides.

"Let's see what kind of ships the Chief has for you," Rufus said.

They stepped inside. The tower was a hollow shaft rising into darkness. Their feet lifted.

Slowly.

Then suddenly they shot upward.

Mari's stomach tried to stay behind.

Their movement ceased in an octagonal room lined with holo displays and wide windows. The translucent floor showed the shaft below, a dizzying drop. Shelves lined two walls, crowded with crystal spheres.

A capybara wearing a captain's hat and a tropical shirt lounged in a hammock like gravity was a suggestion and deadlines were a rumor. Aviator sunglasses rested on the brim of his hat.

"Aloha, new friends and old," the Chief said, rolling out of the hammock. He strutted over and hugged Rufus with easy familiarity. "Looking for a ship for these Fragments, yeah?"

"That is correct," Rufus replied. "Good to see you're well, Chief."

Jerro leaned forward, eyes locked on the shelf. "Those are ships, aren't they?"

"Yep," the Chief said, rummaging. "And Rufus says give you the best one I've got. Something about this mission being important." He elbowed Rufus. "Like they all aren't."

"This one *is* different," Rufus said, and for once he didn't sound playful at all.

Mari stepped closer to Rufus, eyes narrowed. "You keep saying things like that. You have to know something."

Rufus hovered slowly, the room seeming to bend around his certainty. "You will retrieve an artifact. You will travel far and deep, burrowing through time itself." He paused. "In the prime fragmentation of the Burrowing Rodent Empire, a power source was forged. It is said to unlock a weapon capable of ending the hyrax threat for good. We believe it may also be key to repairing the rupture."

Mari's blood went cold. "You just said the Burrowing Rodent Empire. Like what I saw in my dream."

"Yes," Rufus said simply. "Long before your time."

Mari moved to the window and stared down at the dock and the ships. "Follow-up question. You also said, *we*. Who is *we*?"

Before Rufus could answer, the Chief snapped his fingers like he'd just remembered something. "Ah. This is the one you want."

He pulled a crystal sphere from the shelf and tossed it to Jerro.

Jerro caught it clumsily, then held it up to the light. Inside, a miniature ship rotated in slow suspension, sleek and sharp and unreal.

"You'll be the best to use it," the Chief said. "Your engineering talent will guide you."

Rufus gestured toward the center of the room. "Excellent. Let us be on our way."

The Chief's casual grin slipped for a moment. He saluted sharply. Rufus returned it.

"May the threads guide your way, little ones," the Chief said.

As the words left his mouth, gravity took them again. They became weightless, descended the tower, and stepped out onto the dock.

"Jerro and Greg," Rufus said, voice suddenly all command, "prepare the ship. Mari, come with me. I will show you how to navigate the chronoarch."

Jerro looked at Greg with a shaky glare, as though he was about to admit he had no idea how to *prepare a ship.*

Then he looked back at the crystal sphere.

The ship inside it rotated, showing its long sleek hull, the rounded crest running the length. Small spherical bulbs protruded at the front and back. Violet streaks swirled through deep blue, like light trapped beneath ice. Furled sails lay folded into seams along the spine, ornamental more than necessary. Angular wings projected rearward from the sides, flared tips extending beyond the hull. Toward the back sat a horseshoe-shaped cockpit ringed with transparent glass, giving a full field of view.

Jerro, Lunda's voice touched his thoughts. *I was curious if I had predicted correctly that you would be the one to attune.*

Jerro's mind stuttered. *Lunda? Attune to what?*

Attune to me. To the ship. You're the anchor. You can carry my consciousness. Once you pull the ship into being, I will join you there.

Greg poked Jerro's shoulder. "What are you doing, buddy?"

Jerro blinked rapidly.

Then, like his body had done this a thousand times, he threw the sphere out over the void.

The ship sprang into existence at full size, unfolding into the berth and locking into place. A soft pulse rolled through the dock, a ripple of energy that tickled Greg's whiskers and made the fur along Jerro's arms lift.

The ship settled into place with quiet certainty.

"That's awesome," Greg said, and slapped Jerro a quick high five. Not the full routine. Just a clean hit.

Greg, Jerro, and Phlip ran aboard, exploring the ship with the reverent hunger of kids finding a hidden room in their own house.

∞

Rufus and Mari walked toward the partitioned platform they'd arrived on.

"Mari," Rufus said, "this isn't something you learn by forcing it. The chronoarch answers when it wants to. It moves through you. That's one of the reasons you were chosen. The ability is already there, innate and sleeping. We're going to wake it. Are you prepared?"

Mari nodded, nervous enough that her throat felt tight.

A wide copper saucer drifted overhead, blotting out the light as it passed. Half a dozen mice scurried across its back and vanished into a hatch. A ring of windows encircled the top.

Hovering over the sectioned platform, the saucer flickered. It blinked in and out of existence, faster each time.

Then, a vacuuming boom swallowed all light and sound in a radius that reached only to Mari and Rufus's faces.

An instant later, the dock returned. The chatter poured back in.

Mari swallowed. "Is that what happened when we came here?"

"Indeed," Rufus said. "That is what transit looks like to the observer."

Mari stepped onto the divided pad, drawn to it. "How does it work? How do I know where to go?"

"You need not know," Rufus said gently. "You will guide you. Trust yourself."

He circled her like an instructor in a quiet room. "Let it flow through you like your psionics. Let it permeate your being. Your fragmented self will align with the filaments of time."

Mari closed her eyes.

Her mind tried to run away, as it always did. Dreams. The cave. The writing. The Ancients. Her father.

Her mother.

Her heels lifted slightly.

"Mmm," Rufus said with pleased certainty. "Good. You're getting it."

Mari steadied her breath. For a second, the fear didn't vanish, but it stopped biting.

"Alright," Rufus said. "Sever the connection. We will do a full run-through on your ship. Don't be nervous. You're going to be exactly what you need to be."

Mari opened her eyes as her weight returned.

And for the first time she could remember, she felt… at ease.

Not safe. Not certain.

But aligned.

"Now," Rufus said, drifting down the dock toward their ship, "it is time you and your friends made your first autonomous transit."

Mari hurried after him. "Rufus, what if we need help? What if we don't know what we're doing? What if we get lost?"

Rufus didn't slow. "No one is ever lost, and no one knows what to do. That is the glory of it." He glanced back at her. "Trust yourself and trust your friends. They need you, Mari. Whether you realize it or not, you are the leader of this group. You will guide them through whatever waits on the other side."

Mari climbed aboard, breath catching. "Rufus, I'm—"

Jerro popped his head out of the arched control room doorway. "I think we're all ready!"

Mari looked back to Rufus.

He smiled, warm and steady.

Then his voice slid into her mindspace, quiet as a paw on her shoulder.

She is with you. We are with you. She always has been and always will be.

Rufus vanished.

Mari blinked hard. The corner of her eye was wet. She brushed it away with the back of her paw, jaw tightening.

Jerro motioned toward the front station. "Controls are over there. I'm assuming you're flying?"

Mari climbed into the pilot seat and wrapped her paws around the controls. Energy channeled from the ship, interfacing with Mari directly. Greg and Jerro took auxiliary stations behind her, one on each side.

"Alright," Mari said, voice sharper than she felt. "Let's do this."

The takeoff was wobbly. The ship swayed like it were testing her.

Mari steadied it.

The motion came back to her like something remembered in the body, even if she didn't know where the memory lived.

Like riding a bike, her mind offered.

Mari had never ridden a bike. Had never seen one. Had never even heard the word.

But the knowing was there anyway.

"You know we're gonna have to come up with a name for this ship," Greg said as they drifted toward the chronoarch platform, wobble returning.

Mari focused on what Rufus had shown her. She let the feeling rise. Not thought—not logic—flow.

Jerro leaned toward Greg, starting to answer. "How about—"

The space distorted.

Sound thinned and modulated as if it were dropping away.

Station dissolved, and they hurtled into the chromatic waterfall.

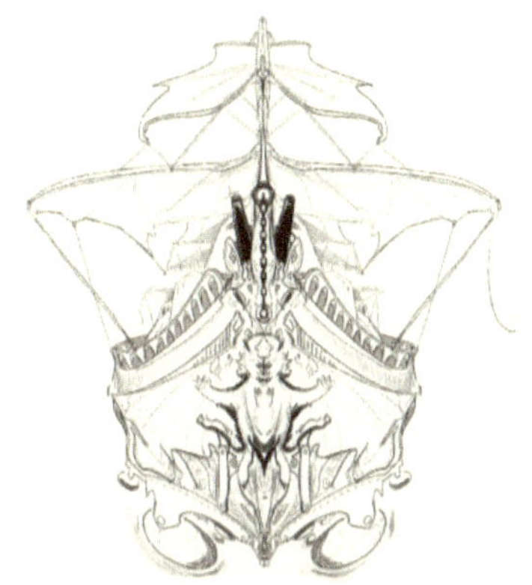

CHAPTER 9 | THE PRINCE

"AAAAAUUUUBERGINE CRUISER?" Jerro's voice finally caught up as they spilled out of the chromatic waterfall that accompanied the chronoarch transit, the sound tugging behind them like a streamer dragging in their wake. A whooshing, percussive rush followed as the world came into focus and the colors found their shapes.

The moment sound and space reconnected, Greg was already out of his chair, making his exit from the cockpit. "That's a terrible name," he said, moving toward the edge of the open-air deck to survey their new surroundings. "You're the only rodent alive that calls it that."

Jerro hopped up and followed him out onto the ship's rough charcoal surface. The deck gripped under his webbed paws. "My grandmother called eggplant that," he shot back. "And look at her. She's purple. She's huge. It fits."

Greg took in the scene as the humid air lapped around him. His fur rippled like grass in the wind. They were flying, a few hundred tails above an ocean of lush foliage, so thick that it took several moments for him to process what he was even looking at. He turned back over his shoulder at Jerro as he approached the smooth railing. A smile washed over Greg's face as his focus slid past Jerro and into the cockpit, to Mari at the controls. She piloted with calm confidence. With little effort, she manipulated an array of holographic controls, the motions practiced and certain, nothing tentative in them. A circlet of pulsating blue light crowned her head. Branches propagated outward, linking with elements in the cockpit, then dissipated.

They flew along the contours of a broad basin lined by short hills, a river threading through it in a wide, twisting channel visible from their elevated position. It emptied into an immense body of water. Over the horizon, a stack of flickering clouds formed a dark thunderhead. The low rumbling of thunder built through their bodies, causing Greg and Jerro's fur to stand on end as a sharp, clean essence graced their nostrils.

After a moment, Jerro broke through the silence. "Where do you think we are?"

Greg turned towards Jerro. "No idea, but it isn't home, and it definitely isn't Station." He repositioned—his tone shifting. "And honestly, I'm relieved."

"Relieved?" Jerro echoed.

"Yeah." Greg kept his eyes on the valley. "For the first time I can remember, I feel free. Free from expectations, the rules. The constant criticism."

"Aren't you a little concerned? We don't know where we are. We don't even know where we just were, really."

"Honestly, Jerro, I'd rather be anywhere with you and Mari than go back to that. I guess…" His voice thinned. "I feel more at home here with you two than I ever did there."

In the distance, there was a break in the canopy, and Greg spotted movement.

Greg flung his paw out beyond the railing. "Look over there!" he pointed out to Jerro, who had been hanging onto Greg's last words.

They set eyes on half a dozen hulking gray-green quadrupedal creatures covered in organic armor plating. Their whiplike tails terminated with a large hammer of a tip. The creatures lumbered about, snapping trees to the forest floor like twigs.

"What in the burrow are those?" Jerro replied.

The ship lurched. A high-frequency tone cut through the whirring wind. All other noise fell off into a dull echo as a wave of force swept over them. Jerro and Greg grasped the railing while the floor beneath them turned to a wall.

"Hang on, boys, we've got a bit of a situation on our paws!" Mari yelled, as the aftershock of the explosion faded out her voice.

The source became apparent as a group of three creatures tore close past the ship, all muscle and forward drive, their bodies heavy and aerodynamic at the same time. Thick, glossy plumage clung to them in layered plates that shifted from a blackened gloss to bruised greens and purples as they banked. Their throats extended in long, sinewy columns, more like flexible stalks than necks, and along each one ran a ridge of stiff quills that lifted into a ragged crest when they turned. Wide-set eyes flashed like wet glass, fixed on the ship with a predator's focus.

They let out a series of trilling screeches that might have sounded almost musical if the notes hadn't fractured into something sharp and hostile. On their backs, blasters protruded from mechanical exoskeletons that cinched tight to their frames. As the creatures passed the ship, the weapon pivoted around with precise, cold control and released another volley. A direct strike to the broadside.

Lunda's calm voice reverberated in their minds, just as it had back on Station.

Initiating reflexive shielding and recommending evasive maneuvers.

"Yeah, no kidding!" Mari said sarcastically, then asked aloud, "Does this thing have any defensive weapons or what?"

Of course, there are manned turrets in the fore and another in the aft of the ship.

A secondary explosion rocked the ship, sending the boys sliding down the railing. This had come from inside the hull.

"Jerro, see if you can run some damage control on that hit we took. Greg, you heard Lunda. Pick a turret and let's make these feathered jerks regret it!" Mari commanded confidently as the nose of the ship lifted to gain altitude.

Jerro's steps felt heavy and sluggish from the added force. With strained effort, he made his way into the ship's interior. Greg, on the other hand, found his way to the forward-positioned turret with ease. He slid into the cushioned seat, where he had a near-full forward view.

Alright, how do I turn this thing on? Greg thought.

Lunda's deadpan reply landed in his mind like it had been there the whole time. *Use your mind clearly.*

Mari cut in before Lunda could add anything else. *Don't be snarky to my friend.* She didn't sound out of breath. She sounded close.

Jerro's thought followed a beat later, strained with effort. *I can hear you both. Also… there's a serious fire down here.*

Fire suppression engaged, Lunda replied. *Portable unit left. Plasma torch and nano patch below.*

Thick mist deployed from a pod that flipped down within a hidden wall panel. Jerro popped open an adjacent cubby and yanked out a canister. Foam leapt from the spout, swallowing the flames. Instantly, the residual smoke got sucked through the breach in the siding.

Thanks, Lunda. I think I've got it from here, Jerro sent, and felt his own tension loosen a notch.

Mari's thought brushed in again, quick and incredulous. *Oh cool, so we're all… telepathically linked?*

She dove the ship to evade another volley.

Lunda answered with the same steady certainty as gravity. *Yes. On Station, you were all attuned to the same psionosol frequency. This allows telepathic communication. My intelligence has been transferred to this ship. I will accompany you on your mission. This is statistically favorable.*

Greg's mouth twitched. "Fantastic." Without moving his body, he whipped the turret around. The formation was locked in an adaptive heads-up display. Greg's focus guided the target acquisition system through the avian aggressors. A rapid series of callouts identified the central target as priority. He channeled his mind blast, which wrapped around the pod and flowed into the turret's focal point. The force split into a barrage of powerful missiles that ripped through the atmosphere, leaving a wake of distorted trace.

Lunda, why are we doing all the work here? Greg sent, more annoyed than afraid. *Isn't there something you can do since you're our guide?*

Lunda's answer arrived flat and immediate. *My core programming limits my ability to cause direct harm. However, I can assist you in causing it. I am providing real-time navigation assistance to Mari through her neural uplink, directing Jerro to ship resources, and aiding you with target discrimination.*

In tight formation, the avian squad turned and dove swiftly, evading Greg's volley. In unison, they returned their own round of blasts towards the cockpit of the ship.

Mari, heads up! Greg shoved the warning into the mindspace.

The ship wrenched into a barrel roll. A success this time. No explosion, but a near miss.

I'm getting set up in the aft turret, Jerro sent, breath tight with effort. *This one has a slide system so I can move across the stern…* His awe slipped through anyway. *This is impressive engineering.*

Lunda cut in before anyone could argue with that. *I've evaluated reasonable outcomes and recommend withdrawal as the best course of action.*

Mari's jaw set. *I can feel her. I know what she can do.*

The vessel whipped around, rotating into an elongated somersault spin and cutting the primary thrusters. As their trajectory came into alignment with the enemy formation, she shifted to full power, adhering the boys to their seats. For the first time, she felt like something wasn't pushing back when she reached for it.

Jerro, starboard, Mari sent. *I've got something in mind.*

She cut the primary thrusters again, and a series of accessory points along the left side radiated an indigo glow. They drifted hard, exposing the entire right side to the birds but simultaneously allowing both turrets to open a full attack. Jerro and Greg let off sequential blasts. The first was dodged. Greg's volley, however, landed squarely on the formation, impacting the central bird. It immediately dropped out of the sky and plummeted towards the jungle canopy, a streamer of smoke indicating its descent.

The remaining two returned a direct round of laser fire. This time, the reflexive shielding spun up and absorbed the blasts as a hexagonal shield pattern emanated, then subsided from the impact point.

As Mari regained control of the ship, Lunda rang through their minds.

Additional enemies approaching from indicated direction.

Simultaneously, Mari caught sight of Lunda's warning in her periphery. Another tight formation of three birds dropped from the cover provided by the thickening sheet of stratocumulus clouds. The formation was too clean. Too deliberate. Whatever these things were, they were hunting them.

Why didn't you let me know sooner? Mari sent, the thought sharp with panic and sharper with herself.

I'm sorry, Mari, Lunda replied. *An advanced signature cloaking masked their position until they broke cover.*

Jerro felt Mari's frustration spike and vanish, leaving something colder behind it.

Their shots were still chasing the last two birds from the first formation when the sky split open. The new formation let out a torrent of laser fire and followed up with an energy ball. The sphere crackled and snapped as it impacted the reflexive shielding. Suddenly it stopped. All forward progress halted. Pulsating energy flickered through the hexagonal shielding, shifting from a gentle blue into a deep violet, then finally transitioning into a dominant red. The orb's progress restarted, and it slipped through the shielding accompanied by a resonating detonation.

Mari was torn from her seat by the blast. Phlip joined her, heaped against the far side of the cockpit. As she stood to survey the damage, a volley of laser fire forced her to take cover behind the control foundation. She could hear the material of the hull splintering in a horrific tearing sound as she avoided the unrelenting salvo.

Mari, I recommend the use of restraint systems in the future. Lunda sent.

Seriously Lunda? I gathered as much. Are you guys okay? Mari sent.

All good up here, Greg sent back. *Or… down? We're dropping. Fast.*

Gravity shifted, and Mari slid towards the front of the flight deck.

I'm all in one piece, I think, Jerro sent, strained. *What was that?*

Lunda's answer came crisp, but not cold. *Energy readings indicate the reflexive shielding was penetrated by a quantum pulsar. Engines are disabled. Recommend bracing for impact in approximately thirteen seconds.*

Lunda's voice began to count down as a redundant red light source took over, illuminating the interior of the ship.

Greg's laugh came out thin. *Well. This was fun.*

Jerro gripped the sides of the seat. *Mari, why? Why didn't you listen?*

Hold on! Not yet! Mari sent back, determination seeping through.

Mari grabbed Phlip as the ship's free fall accelerated. Greg and Jerro checked their restraints and prepared for impact. Greg's view became a rapidly approaching array of vine-laden treetops. Jerro stared into the darkening sky. Fat drops of rain began to splat against the translucent capsule. Keeping their distance, the two formations of long-necked birds circled the trail of impending wreckage like vultures.

Mari wrestled the controls, attempting to regain power and command of the ship. Her efforts were futile.

Greg watched, helpless, as the ship pierced into the jungle like a knife driving into its target. His face wrinkled and eyes narrowed. Frantically, he grasped at the tight straps that swept over his shoulders and down his broad chest, fastening him into the seat. The curved window on the turret cracked as branches impacted and broke under the ship. The jungle floor came into view. Vines snapped and whipped in a chaotic cacophony, followed by a burst of sound so intense it resonated through the ship and slowly dissipated.

In an instant, it all stopped.

Greg's eyes were closed by now, and as he slowly opened them he realized they had yet to hit the ground, but were close enough that he watched a long orange insect with thousands of legs scurry across the jungle floor.

The ship began reversing, pulling out of the shattered mess of trees and foliage just how it had entered.

Lunda, Mari. Greg's thought snapped tight with disbelief. *Are you doing this? What's happening?*

I don't think it was me, Mari sent, and the uncertainty in it made Greg's stomach turn.

Lunda's reply came fast, threaded with alert. *Anomalous energy source detected in close proximity. Emergency systems override in effect. Extreme caution advised.*

As they came to a soft hover above the canopy, they saw it. A figure suspended in the air, with the appearance of a large marmot, hind paws floating weightlessly and a long dark cloak lofting in the developing wind. Its eyes glowed a bright purple. A polearm weapon slung on its back and a light yet well-fitted armored chest piece graced its torso. A paw extended, clenched in a fist, mirrored the movement of their ship with seemingly little effort.

Mari sent it before she could stop herself. *You seeing this?*

Yep. Jerro's reply was clipped.

Greg said nothing, still reeling from his headfirst death dive.

Mari exited the cockpit and positioned herself on the deck, Phlip at her side. She smiled, unsure if it would even be seen at this distance, and produced a hesitant wave towards the stranger.

In an instant, it gestured with its free paw and projected a powerful mind blast that tore at Mari. She dropped for cover with her back to the lower solid portion of the railing. The blast ripped overhead and over the roof of the cockpit. It impacted the central bird from the approaching trio that had downed their ship.

Mari peeked her head over the railing and saw two heavy powered suits now flanking the stranger. Each hovered on small thrusters mounted along the limbs, with three larger jets on the back. Marred with soot and grime, the alabaster armor had lost whatever luster it once held, fading against the ashen sky. Their mirrored visors lifted as they appeared to confer with the cloaked figure. From her position, Mari caught a flicker of rough fur shifting behind the helmet glass, but the rest was lost to distance.

The visors dropped. The suits split in opposing directions, and dual cannons deployed over their broad, plated shoulders. Mari watched each armored figure surge toward the now-reduced bird formations. The ship lurched beneath her as it began moving again over the jungle.

With a light thud, the ship came to a halt, and Mari looked over the edge again to see they had landed safely in a small glade. A cacophony of cawing erupted from the trees as colorful birds flocked to the cloud-covered sky. The space stilled, and foreign sounds poured back in at a steady pace while the rainfall created a percussive backdrop.

Without a sound, the cloaked figure landed on the deck of the ship near Mari. She could make out details now. This was definitely a burrowing rodent, but its appearance was uncanny, not marmot, gopher or prairie dog but a combination of all, without resembling any distinctly. Its cloak was soaked and hung heavily. The ends were frayed and tattered from wear.

In a warbled and unintelligible language, which echoed into Mari's mind, it attempted to communicate, but was unsuccessful. It reached up to its temple and attached a small disc device and rotated it, as if it was tuning a dial.

"How's this?" He asked. "Can you understand me now?"

Mari took a step closer, Phlip hanging tight to her side. "Yeah. I can."

The stranger did not move. His voice projected with commanding resonance and calm pacing. "Excellent. I'm Lukyaza, Prince of the Borruki. Sovereign Watcher of this sector."

Mari noticed a knot in her throat and forced out a reply. "Nice to meet you, Prince Lukyaza." She paused awkwardly, his calm gaze patiently locked on her.

"I'm Mari Stonepaw. From… The Burrow." she said with a blushing smile. "I think."

She broke eye contact and quickly searched around for something else to add to the conversation.

"Oh, and this is Phlip!" Phlip stared off into the jungle, unaware of the life-threatening peril that had just transpired.

Greg and Jerro emerged from the access point near the flight deck, which led into the ship's interior. They hustled across the deck and joined Mari and Phlip.

The armored suits landed hard on the deck. Their plating was charred from energy impacts, and one struggled to lift an arm that had been disabled. Scratches and scars ran across the faded surfaces—some fresh, some aged.

The suits unfurled and opened smoothly from the front as the creatures climbed out. Like Lukyaza, their otherworldly appearance was both unsettling and striking — the kind of form that felt quintessentially burrowing rodent, distilled into something too perfect.

Space held between the groups as they continued to inspect each other. Mari noticed a simple black-and-white crest on the left breast of each chest piece. It was outlined by a braided circle, and within it, a single hollow triangle lay upside down, overlapping the braid.

She narrowed in on the Prince and could see his paw trembling under the folds of his lightly layered armor. He caught her attention and clasped his paws behind his back in a natural movement.

Mari stepped forward. "Well, Lukyaza, Prince of the Borruki, where are we?"

Lukyaza cocked his head slowly and narrowed his eyes. "This is system three-one-nine, a unitary star system, and we are on the third major celestial body from the central star."

160

CHAPTER 10 | ANUNNA

Nightfall enveloped the downed ship, now turned makeshift campsite. A cooling breeze provided relief from the oppressive humidity that had blanketed the jungle. The sky cleared, save for a smattering of thin clouds. The partial moon illuminated the edges of those nearby, highlighting them in a soft silvery glow. Prince Lukyaza had introduced his two companions, Guardians Natal and Maxuun. They sat on a moss-covered log, which lay on the jungle floor adjacent to a small campfire. In turn, the three friends shared their names, and Mari introduced Phlip.

The Guardians' suits were now powered down and situated near a large tree overgrown with thick vines. They wore loose tan and white uniforms and seemed to be refrained in conversation despite Jerro and Greg's attempts to get them to open up.

Jerro had made his way back to the ship, guided by Lunda. On first request, she had agreed to guide him through the mechanics that underpinned the ship's operation. The familiarity of her voice grounded him in this hostile world. A muffled ratcheting or metal clank would emanate from the interior periodically.

Hovering lights patrolled silently through the periphery of the site. They flickered in and out of view between the towering vegetation. These were security drones. The Guardians had deployed them after a thorough reconnaissance of the area.

Greg rifled through his bag and produced several slices of pizza. They were cold and held their shape well. He passed one to Mari. Greg offered the Prince and Guardians some, which they had respectfully declined. Greg and Mari looked at each other and rotated the triangular cheese-covered bread in paw.

Mari looked up at Greg. "Do you think we start from the tip or this thick end?"

Greg rolled his into a cylinder and presented it to Mari. "You could do this!"

"I'm not sure about that Greg, but don't let me stop you," she replied, and started gnawing at the crust. It was cold and stubborn, more chew than flavor, like it didn't want to be eaten.

Phlip lay on his stomach near the fire and grazed through foliage on the jungle floor. His attention caught on a patch of especially good vegetation, and he settled in, taking quick, successive bites.

Mari swallowed and looked to Lukyaza, who had been observing their pizza experience. "Prince Lukyaza, what are you and the Guardians doing here?"

"We are on a mission." He paused briefly and glanced at Maxuun and Natal. They were within earshot but preoccupied with maintaining their suits. "We are in search of an ancient—" his jaw tightened, "—relic that was said to be hidden in these hills millions of years ago when our people first settled this system."

"We're actually looking for a key," Greg said quickly, then glanced at Mari. "Kind of."

Mari pierced him with a quick glare. "Yeah, but I'm not sure where to start. We don't even know exactly how we got here."

The prince examined them both for a moment, his eyes narrowed. "Where exactly did you say you came from?"

"Well… it's hard for me to fully understand the last few lunes. But, we call our home The Burrow," Mari explained.

The Prince stared into the night sky, studying the moon. "Interesting. Does it feel familiar?" He gestured toward the moon.

Mari and Greg matched Lukyaza's focus. Their investigation quickly revealed the answer. The silent, luminous sphere hung overhead, surrounded by a spray of bright stars. Its silver surface was scarred with dark craters, breaking any uniform appearance. This was the same moon they'd watched through The Spine's opening back home, lune after lune. This was their planet. They were where they had always been. Greg and Mari locked wide eyes, clearly having the same realization.

Their surprise shifted to Lukyaza, who now stood with lips forming a barely perceptible smile. "You are in a familiar place, but an unfamiliar time, I think."

The two guardians chatted quietly off to the side in their layered alien language. They moved back and forth to the suits, tinkering and making minor adjustments. At one point, they opened a panel in the back of a helmet, revealing a compartment that ejected three parabolic discs. They rearranged them and slid them back into place. Every few minutes they scanned the group around the fire, then returned to their work.

"Tell me, what is your memory of this world?" The Prince asked.

"Well, we actually didn't leave home a lot," Mari started.

Greg quickly interrupted. "Some of us didn't leave home much."

Mari rolled her eyes and continued. "The Burrow was our safe haven, and the world outside… it *is—was—will be* ruled by dangerous creatures. Sort of like those birds we just fought, but without the weapons and tech. Also, giant insects and… well, I've never seen them, but we learned about others that lived their entire life under water. Our community was forced into hiding during the war with the birds." She trailed off after the last line, her eyes losing focus on the Prince.

"And that's about all we know. We've lived our entire lives in The Burrow," Greg picked up and rounded off Mari's explanation.

"Wait," Jerro cut into the conversation. He must have been standing there for a while listening, or at least long enough to put the pieces together. "We never left?"

Without a word, Greg got up and placed an arm around his friend. They sat down again next to Mari, who had shifted down the mossy log to make room.

Lukyaza registered the details they shared and returned his gaze to the moon. "Fascinating. I do have a theory that might explain how you ended up here. For millennia, our engineers and scientists have been working to bridge temporal space. They have never been completely successful. Only glimpsing time in shards… like looking through layers of broken glass and trying to discern the image on the other end. There was always a key element missing, a link."

The Prince landed the last line squarely on Mari. Her eyes darted left then right, searching for anything but herself he may have been referring to. She was the only option.

"You think I'm that link?"

Lukyaza's eyes lingered on her, then he turned away. He continued pacing slowly around the fire. Reaching out with his paw, he traced the stars. Glowing particulates lifted from his claws. It formed a three-dimensional visual field that reflected Prince Lukyaza's words. His recount swam into illustration. Behind it, the dense jungle flickered in the campfire light. The sky opened into an ocean, divided by a milky river.

"We come from a place far from this one, but not dissimilar. Long ago, our scientists developed a technology that allowed the instantaneous navigation of space. This opened the opportunity for our species to travel vast distances through space." The particulate morphed into three parabolic spacecraft set against a large marbled sphere. Elongated metallic spheres moved silently against a backdrop of violet swirls that sat above deep coral-hued masses. A layered ring fitted around the planet. The colors shifted from white to yellow, then back to white. In a blinding flash, a rift formed ahead, pulling the ships through.

"More challenging though, and what I believe you three have done, is to bridge time." The image shifted, showing their slim purple vessel. The scene pulled back until their ship turned into a dot. It hovered above a line, a simplified representation of time. A diagram traced their jump. The dot moved against the line, indicating backwards travel.

Jerro raised his paw. He quickly realized this was unnecessary and asked his question. "So, The Burrow doesn't exist now?"

"Correct. Your home is yet to be," the Prince answered.

Jerro sat with that response for a moment. His focus locked on the low flames. "How will we be able to get back home then?"

Lukyaza lingered on the question, then redirected with his own. "Did your vessel originate from this, Burrow?"

"No, we came fr—" Jerro was interrupted by Mari.

"We found the ship. It was…" She hesitated. "It was underground, in a cave near The Burrow."

Jerro and Greg shifted their eyes towards her and nodded.

The Prince surveyed the three of them carefully. A natural agreement of sound had organically arisen. The crackling fire served as the percussive framework. Alien croaking and trilling created an omnipresent hum. A distant snap echoed, a tree limb being sheared. The soundscape pulsed, rising to a crescendo and then settling again in a calm rhythm.

Prince Lukyaza looked back at the moon and carried on with his history lesson. "When my progenitors came here those millions of years ago, however, they did not come alone. They had been embroiled in an endless faction war that was carried from our home system, Anunna." The alien starships appeared again, this time engaged in battle. Smaller, agile fighters spun the space between into a spiderweb of dogfights. The scene was swept away in an explosion. All-consuming, it transformed the stellar battlefield into glowing hulks of drifting ash.

"We sought to escape this cycle of war and start anew. Our faction, known as the Borruki, were first to this world. A forward expedition brought the single moon during the primordial era. This moon stabilized the planet and protected it from external forces. It was a shield to allow evolution to take its course." A group of Borruki gathered around a control panel set against a large rectangular window with rounded corners. Outside, the gray barren landscape gave way to darkness. A partial sphere emerged. White wisps swirled against a deep cerulean backdrop. Verdant green masses broke against the sea of blue.

"Their effort was to guide the inevitable growth of life within this infantile system. We settled many of the nearby celestial bodies, but this planet, already teeming with life, held significance. Beyond the moon, every effort was made not to interfere with the natural order. Our scrolls had foretold of a world that would one day become a sanctuary for the Borruki but that any direct interference would disrupt that fate." Terraced buildings organically integrated with the landscape. A small elongated disk zipped by, rotated and docked onto the side. The scene transitioned to a crowded market brimming with chatter. The Borruki were shown living in peace, in harmony with the order of the world.

"The original Borruki had attempted to hide the quantum signature from their folding wake; however, they were unsuccessful. All four factions made their way here in time, following the remains of that signature. Like a trail through the stars." The display shifted. Three distinct vessels loomed across the same coral and violet mottled orb as the Borruki ship had. The first was a wide, flattened triangle with jagged, extended tips. Second was a network of smaller corvettes that moved in unison. The last starship was tall and rectangular, composed of smaller blocks that undulated in a slow, breathing rhythm.

Mari jumped in without hesitation. "So, if they followed the Borruki here… how can we be sure that we won't be next?"

Lukyaza was quiet for a long moment. "We cannot be sure, only vigilant." His distant gaze shifted from Mari back to the projection. "We buried our wake as deeply as we knew how. However, time has a way of eroding even the best burrow."

He shifted back to his lecture. "The combatants you just encountered are the Aviaki, feathered and capable combatants. What we fought was a scouting party. They are honorable, unlike the others, and adhere to the non-interference treaty. I believe they are searching for the same relic as my team." A life-size version of the

Aviaki stood frozen before them now. The form rotated around a central axis to give the friends a full view of the enemy they had fought earlier. A small head sat atop a noodle-like neck. A slim, rounded beak protruded from lifeless eyes. Layers of small dark feathers formed a sleek coat, while larger snowy plumage extended from its hidden frame. Holding this monstrosity up were two bare and pale yellowed feet. Like sticks propping up a skyscraper.

"The second to come here were the Grishki, creatures exhibiting a reversal of typical anatomy, with exoskeletons and decentralized neural structures. Finally, the Ninurki arrived, with cold running blood, scaled skin and an insatiable desire for power." A representative figure for each of these descriptions rotated in succession.

Lukyaza walked around the projected images of each of these faction creatures as he continued his explanation. The glowing particulate morphed and continued to illustrate his story.

"In Anunna, the factions battled on a massive scale. Fleets of starships destroyed and entire planets won and lost in single battles, millions of lives lost. The cost to all factions was immense. Now, this planet has become nothing but a new front in this endless war, a sandbox where the factions experiment with new techniques to dispatch each other, but on a smaller and more… intimate scale."

He paused and stared through the flames of the fire as they licked the night sky. His eyes reflected the flames as Mari, Jerro and Greg waited for the story to continue. The wood popped, kicking Lukyaza out of his trancelike state.

"What faction were those giant creatures with the armored backs?" Jerro asked.

Lukyaza focused on Jerro. "Where exactly did you see them?"

"When we first, uh… arrived here, Greg and I spotted them in an open field. A small herd, maybe twenty or so." He looked at Greg for approval, which he gave with a nod.

"Ah, I see. This planet was not a blank slate, and by the time our follow-on forces arrived, life had already been flourishing here, assuming the same archetypical forms associated with our factions. In all our travels through the universe, we have identified a trend among celestial bodies of this type. They always produce the same fundamental design of life, as form follows function. Even on this planet, the same fundamental forms have evolved separately after mass extinction events reset the cycle." The images shifted to a time-lapse of the planet evolving. Single-celled organisms swimming shifted to larger, more complex life forms that moved to land. The flora and fauna shifted as eons passed before their eyes.

"So they aren't of any faction?" Greg confirmed with Lukyaza.

"Correct, those creatures are endemic to this planet, indigenous organisms," Lukyaza responded.

Mari interrupted again. "Your mistake… the Borruki's mistake, is the reason the war was brought here?"

"Unfortunately, you are correct, Mari. Clarity in hindsight does not absolve responsibility. This conflict spread to this system through my faction. The cycle will continue long after I cease to exist."

"What even is the point of this war?"

"What is the point of any war?" He stared into the flames. "Fear. Fear is very good at convincing itself it is necessary. Once war becomes the lens through which survival is understood, then everything becomes justified. Resources. Ideology. Merely existing. Now they seek to find the meaning of this place, interpreting the scrolls for their own agendas. Generation after generation of my bloodline sought to protect this sanctuary, but fate is inevitable. The scrolls did not cause this conflict. We did. Now we cling to them, hoping meaning might excuse the damage."

"What exactly do you mean by the scrolls?" Jerro inquired.

"It's a bit of a misnomer—they are not actually written scrolls, but data storage devices, capable of tapping into void space. When the first Borruki came to this system, they crafted a set of scrolls that are said to grant the interpreter great knowledge and power. Originally they were held within the Thaullic Vault, located at the original outpost of the Borruki." Lukyaza gestured at the moon and continued, "However, they were stolen many years ago, long before my memory. We've only recovered two, and without the entire set they are incoherent at best."

Greg leaned over towards Mari and whispered, "Do you think these scrolls could be the key we're looking for?"

"Could be?" she answered, truly unsure.

Lukyaza reached out a paw, returning the glowing particulate. "That's enough for tonight. We've got a long day ahead of us tomorrow."

"Lukyaza, what do you know about the hyrax?" Mari asked suddenly.

The Prince turned back towards Mari—muscle in his jaw shifting. "The what? I'm not sure the translator picked that up?"

"The hyrax," Mari firmly repeated.

"Hmm, you're saying h-y-r-a-x?" His brow tightened. "I've no record of it."

Mari, Jerro and Greg all looked at each other, unsure of this response. Lukyaza sensed the unease and drove the conversation forward. "At sunrise, Natal, Maxuun and I will head out to trace a signal we picked up in the hills not far from here. You are welcome to join us. After we investigate the signal, we can bring your ship back to our forward outpost. Our mechanics should be able to make repairs."

"Well, it's not like we have much else going on," Greg said in response, and Mari and Jerro nodded in agreement.

"Let us all get some rest then. Good night to you all. It was a pleasure to converse. The Guardians will take watch tonight. Their drones can interface with them while asleep and will alert them of any danger." The Prince gave a small bow and deployed an elevated platform, which expanded and hovered. It then expanded slightly more as if it was taking a breath and opened at one end, exposing a small but comfortable chamber where the Prince climbed in. Natal and Maxuun had already deployed similar sleeping pods.

The three friends and Phlip went back to the ship where they had a small bunk room. It was uneven as the ship was merely sitting on the jungle floor, without any sort of landing gear deployed, but it would work for the night. The beds were surprisingly comfortable for their modest appearance. Phlip found a spot on one of the bottom bunks, and Mari climbed atop. Greg and Jerro took a set of bunks just on the other side of the tight space. Two empty bunks lined the back wall, which curved slightly as it flowed into the ceiling.

Rest cycle initiated. Lunda's even voice flowed in and the lighting dimmed. *Good night.*

Jerro lay on his back, paws folded across his chest. After a moment, he spoke, not aloud. *Thanks Lunda. For earlier. For… watching the angles, we couldn't.*

There was a brief pause before she responded. *Of course, Jerro, that is my function.* Silence followed.

Mari shifted in her bunk, the faint creak of the frame the only sign of her movement. She stared at the curved ceiling, replaying the way the battle went in her head. The way Jerro's voice had sounded when he asked why she hadn't listened.

Greg rolled onto his side, facing the wall. "Freedom's louder than I thought," he mumbled. "Hard to sleep in all that noise."

Jerro didn't answer.

Mari swallowed. The hum of the ship felt different now, less like momentum, more like a held breath. A welling in her throat. She closed her eyes, telling herself she'd chosen action because someone had to. *Was it fear?* Her thoughts shifted to the Prince's explanation of war.

The thought unraveled before it finished. Darkness pressed in, warm and heavy. The floor seemed to tilt as something ancient took shape behind her eyes.

∞

Mari stood at the edge of a large circular open-air structure. Tall white stone columns ringed the space, their surfaces worn smooth with age.

The sky glowed amber—the sun fixed low on the horizon. Bleached steps descended from where she stood, leading down to cracked earth that stretched outward until it met a line of shadowed mountains.

Without meaning to, Mari tilted her head, her deep eyes drawn inward toward the center of the marbled temple.

The floor was segmented into radial partitions that joined at a single point, like the chronoarch pad from Station. But this surface was different—ornate. Inlaid with a mosaic that caught the light in subtle shifts. As she examined it, the pattern stopped reading like decoration. It suggested structure. Lines connected points in ways that felt intentional, branching and rejoining, looping back on themselves before breaking off again. There were no clear coastlines, no familiar borders, only regions implied by density and angle, and routes that seemed to slip through blank tiles as if the surface were marking something that didn't quite sit in the same place as everything else.

A distant rumbling interrupted her focus.

Wind tore through the columns, kicking dust into the air as the sky darkened. Mari grabbed a nearby pillar as the ground trembled beneath her. A curtain of clouded debris advanced from every direction, swallowing the horizon.

She turned back towards the center. The floor shifted. Stone plates separated and folded inward, opening slowly into a vast black void.

Panic surged. She had only moments.

From the darkness below, something rose.

The crown of a tree emerged first. Arresting her completely. It was immense and impossibly beautiful, embodying all four seasons at once. One side stood barren and skeletal. Another overflowed with green life. Between them, buds blossomed into flowers and leaves burned into autumn color.

The trunk followed, driving deep roots into a floating mass of rock that ascended from the open floor.

Mari looked back.

The sky was gone. The storm had erased all remaining light.

Above her, the temple ceiling fractured. Stone tore apart and collapsed inward. Sand lashed her face, forcing her eyes nearly shut.

The pull returned. Stronger now.

She didn't hesitate.

Three quick steps. A leap.

The world around her collapsed into darkness as her paw closed around a thick root extending from beneath the floating island.

The noise vanished. Silence. Stillness.

Mari hung suspended above the void, stars and celestial objects illuminating the surrounding space. The same endless expanse she had seen before. The ceiling from Station.

She felt unnaturally small. Like a single grain of sand. Yet connected to a part of something vast.

Whole.

CHAPTER 11 | SIGNAL

Good morning. Minor activity detected in the vicinity. Lunda's voice rolled through their groggy minds.

A loud explosion rocked the ship. Enough to shift the three sleeping friends in their beds, ensuring they were awake.

Greg rolled his legs over the edge of the bed and sat up yawning. "What's going on?"

Mari was already on her feet, tightening the straps on Phlip's harness. His lazy cooperation made this more difficult than usual. "I'm not sure, but we'd better get out there and see." She pulled the length of leather firmly through a brass buckle.

Jerro lay motionless, eyes fixed on the ceiling. "Do you think we are going to have even one relaxing moment ever again?"

Greg hopped down from the top bunk, his mass landing next to Jerro. He reached into Jerro's bunk, giving him some playful jabs in the ribs. Jerro squirmed, attempting to avoid Greg's onslaught.

"Guys, stop messing around, this—" Mari froze as she approached the door.

Quiet. Something's out there, Mari sent.

Greg and Jerro froze, their ears shifting to pick up any trace.

Moving away. I think. Mari added.

Greg and Jerro eased towards the door, joining Mari and Phlip.

Lunda. Intel? Jerro sent.

Lunda answered immediately. *At least two unknown life forms aboard the ship. Additional signatures in the vicinity. Sensor damage limiting external readings. Extreme caution advised.*

On your tail, Greg sent, giving a firm nod as his eyes narrowed.

Mari opened the door onto the deck. A dense fog blanketed the jungle now, rolling over the ship's deck in waves. Strewn out clouds were painted fuchsia by the sunrise, gradually forcing out the deep blue of night.

Across the far side of the ship, a large, gray, scaled beast with scattered colorful feathers stood on its thick hind legs. On its back rode a tan stick figure. Two slender legs wrapped down around the sides of the mount. Another set of thin appendages grasped curved metallic rings protruding from a neck harness. A third pair of arms hung loosely, awaiting their purpose.

They had seen this creature before. Last night, in Lukyaza's projection.

A Grishki.

The Grishki guided its mount to the edge of the canted deck. It reached a pincer-like claw down out of sight and produced a small translucent cube. In a single motion, it activated the device with a whir and hurled it towards the campsite below.

Mari reached into her bag and withdrew the petrified watermelon half. Already in motion, she slid the helmet onto her head and threw a leg over Phlip's broad back.

The cube hit the ground below, and an intense buzz filled the air. A shockwave ripped through the quiet fog. The Guardians shot into the sky at high speed, momentarily clearing the haze and leaving a trail in their wake. The stick creature let out an escalating array of chitters in rapid succession from its scissored mandibles. This was a command. A swarm of insects bloomed from the side of the ship where the cube had impacted. The horde swam upwards, undulating under the audible signals from its master.

Rhythmic pulses rolled outward. The cloud of insects, acting as a medium, quivered on the waves. The swarm froze, then dropped out of sight, hard bodies striking the jungle floor like a smattering of rain.

Anomalous electromagnetic readings detected in the atmosphere, Lunda sent.

Jerro reached for Mari. *Hang on Mari, Lunda is picking something up.*

Mari was already in motion, urging Phlip forward with a quick kick of her heels, they took off towards the mounted foe. She focused her energy into a mind blast. Copper flooded her tongue as pressure cinched behind her eyes. Static crackled, arcing and snapping. A final chill coursed through her body, causing her fur to stand on end.

She meant to shape it—to decide. Instead, it surged up too fast, slipping past her control like a reflex, and the realization hit half a second too late. Whatever she sent out, she couldn't take back.

With a thunderous boom, she issued a blast. Splitting the fog and causing it to mushroom outward, rolling over itself like a tidal wave.

The stick creature turned its head in an instant, and its beady eyes drew on Mari. The blast overwhelmed the creature. It tried to move, but it was too late. The rider and the mount froze. Their forms crumbled into fine dust. Overpressure from the blast carried the molecules swirling into the air.

Distant explosions and blaster fire could be heard in the sky above. Mari looked up and squinted. The two guardians were fighting several creatures at a high altitude.

Over the starboard edge of the ship, muffled metal clanking and successive rustling could be heard. Discharges of energy reverberated through the ship. The fog flashed, catching light from the flash in the dim morning light.

Mari, look out! Jerro sent.

A barrage of laser fire impacted her from the opposite side of the ship as three large flying insects landed. Their quad translucent wings distorted the surrounding air. An array of cybernetic enhancements formed around their meager frames. Adding to their appendages, the layer of tech articulated independently. A smattering of weaponry, shielding and alien transmitters moved fluidly with their advance.

Instead of tearing through Mari and Phlip, a field of raw energy absorbed the blaster fire. Mari looked back at the door that led to the ship's interior—Jerro and Greg were approaching her position. Jerro was holding a paw to his temple, focusing on Mari and Phlip. She could hear the light humming of an energy barrier as the frequency modulated at each point to absorb the laser blasts.

Thanks buddy, Mari sent, relief bleeding into her voice.

Without a word, Greg was already charging at high speed. His acceleration shifted the ship underpaw. Enough to cause Jerro to drop to a knee.

He connected with the first cyborg insect and broke it in half, leaving the legs standing in place. The impact sent wire, chitin and metal reeling across the deck. His follow-through continued into the neighboring bug. A cylindrical tube deployed over the arthropod's shoulder. It hummed into a glow, then vanished, along with the attacker.

Greg's momentum carried through the blank space where the creature had disappeared. The third assailant lifted off the deck. Regaining his balance, Greg leapt through the air as the insect let off a hurried shot that grazed past his head and into the jungle beyond. He tackled it midair and took them both overboard, disappearing from Mari and Jerro's view.

Mari stiffened, her pupils dilated, and she slid off Phlip's back. She hit the deck, helmet first, and crumpled into a ball. The bug had reappeared next to Phlip. A syringe deployed around its abdomen from one of the cybernetic arms positioned where Mari had sat.

Jerro faced them and focused on the mind of the insect. He struggled to orient himself with the decentralized neural anatomy. It was a puzzle, an enigma.

Permission to interface, Jerro? Lunda sent, quieter than before. *I can help you map it.*

Jerro didn't hesitate. His brow eased, and Lunda flowed in—gentle where she could have been forceful—and they connected to the alien brain. This wasn't one mind. It was a network. Billions of connected minds formed a singular consciousness. Together, Lunda and Jerro isolated this individual and supplanted a suggestion. Just as he had trained.

The idea was simple—*surrender*. It worked. The bug retracted its arm cannon and folded both legs in a kneel, showing its intent.

Its head dissolved into a pile of chartreuse paste as a blast ripped from above.

Guardian Maxuun landed with a resounding thud on the deck.

"We can't take prisoners." Maxuun said plainly as Jerro shot a look of bewilderment and indignation.

Jerro looked at Maxuun and then at Mari's limp body. Without a word, the Guardian approached Mari and effortlessly lifted her limp body over his shoulder.

"What did it do to her? Will she be okay?" Jerro questioned the Guardian.

Maxuun rotated towards Jerro. "She will be, but we need to get her to Prince Lukyaza immediately. The Grish use a nasty neuro-toxin to incapacitate."

"You didn't have to kill it." Jerro kept his voice level. "I had it."

Maxuun ignored Jerro's concern and made his way towards the now silent camp below. "Come, we must move quickly. Others will be upon us shortly."

In a massive bound, Greg leapt back up to the deck from the side of the ship where he had taken the creature overboard and landed, skidding a few tail lengths before coming to a stop.

Greg smirked. "Guys… I think the ice cream is kicking in." His expression dropped and eyes widened when he saw Mari hung lifeless over the Guardian's armored plate.

Guardian Maxuun and the gang of friends descended from the ship and approached the campsite where Prince Lukyaza had been fighting. The swarm lay in a ring now, motionless and piled around the extinguished fire. Green and yellow entrails marked the remains of a fight. A freshly charred hole graced Lukyaza's cloak, and crimson blood dripped from his clenched paw. Guardian Natal landed softly next to the Prince while Maxuun placed Mari onto a nearby bed of moss. They shared a few concise words in their native language. Natal shared a quick, measured look with Maxuun as their visors deployed. One after the other, they shot into the atmosphere.

The Prince quickly approached Mari as Jerro, Greg and Phlip closed the circle.

He pulled a small hexagonal pouch from inside his cloak, unfastened a loop and opened it, exposing a silvery powder. It moved with a microcurrent within the container. His arm trembled as blood pooled and slid back down the sleeve. With his other paw, he dipped a clawed finger in. The silvery powder swirled around his broken claw. With a smooth motion, he placed it under Mari's nose and snapped. The particles aerosolized, and a moment later, Mari's eyes opened wide.

The Prince placed a paw on her chest as she tried to sit up. "Slowly."

Mari let out a grunt and sputtered. She tried to move her mouth, but a froth of saliva was all she could produce.

"You will need some time to recover, Mari. The toxin is potent. Our antidote opens the body to clear it naturally."

"The Guardians are going to move ahead to the location where we have been tracking the energy signature. I will join the three of you on foot. It isn't far from here — we should be there within half the day. Grab any gear you need and secure your ship, for we may not be back until tomorrow. We depart momentarily." Prince Lukyaza commanded without waiting for questions or response.

"Wait, why can't you just fly us all over there like you did with the ship?" Jerro asked as the Prince began gathering his gear and tending to his own wound.

"For one, my power is not endless. Restraint is wisdom. And that brings me to my second point." Lukyaza's gaze held on Mari a moment longer.

"Let's go. I'll grab our packs and we can get moving," Greg said, already turning back toward the ship.

Jerro felt Lunda's presence brush the edge of his thoughts. *You should remove the energy core before you leave the ship. It will reduce the risk of tampering or theft.*

Oh. Can you guide me to it? Jerro sent.

Of course.

Lunda led him through the ship's inner corridors until they reached a compact engine space. At its center, a spherical object hovered in concentric rings of energy, radiating a hot white glow. A deep, rhythmic bass thumped through the walls, synced to the pulsing field.

You'll need to shut down the phase-reduction fields before you can retrieve it, Lunda sent.

Then, quieter. *Jerro.*

He paused with his paw hovering near the controls. *Yeah?*

When you de-energize the core, my operation will cease.

Jerro swallowed. *Hey. Don't worry. I won't leave you behind. I promise.*

Thank you Jerro. I trust you will keep the core safe and, in turn, me.

Lunda walked Jerro through the sequence. Jerro felt the void that was the shared mindspace. It was empty now. Lunda was gone. The sphere landed in a small cradle, clearly intended for this purpose.

A hatch opened, and lively electronic dance music filled the engine room. Five small hamsters emerged slowly from the sphere. "Greetings, is everything okay out here?" They all said in unison.

"Uh yeah," Jerro responded and continued, "You guys are the energy core?"

"Yes! We're Derf One through Derf Five, and we power the ship!" The five of them chirped together.

Jerro bent over and peered into the sphere's open hatch. Similar to their residence back on Station, the space was significantly larger than the exterior of the object implied. Inside the sphere, Jerro could see three small wheels, sized perfectly for the hamsters, which were still spinning slowly from residual motion. The walls of the interior were lined with lighting that matched the beat of the music. Another hamster was stationed at a table full of controls and buttons. It waved at Jerro.

"That's Derf Prime. She controls things in here." The chorus of Derfs echoed.

"I'm supposed to take the core with me. Um… is that okay with you guys?" Jerro asked the Derfs.

They all looked at each other and at Derf Prime back inside the sphere. "Yeah sure! We'll just be in here, and when you're ready to start things up again, let us know!" said the Derfs with exuberance as they scurried back into the sphere. The hatch snapped closed.

Jerro grabbed the sphere and tucked it securely into his pack.

The group set off through the jungle. It was already getting hot out despite being early morning. The air was thick, and their fur quickly became damp from brushing through the massive dew-covered leaves and thick vines. Colorful flowers opened throughout the jungle, dotting the deep green. Screeches, skittering, and distant snaps echoed while howling and deep guttural calls filled the air as they hiked their way up the hillside.

Prince Lukyaza led the way, clearing foliage as needed with his polearm. Phlip followed closely, carrying Mari on his back. Jerro and Greg took up the rear. Greg didn't like being in the back. He kept turning around, jaw tight, shoulders tense, like he was waiting for the jungle to tap him on the spine. It never did. His nerves didn't seem to care.

The foliage began thinning, and the air became easier to breathe as a light breeze picked up. They were gaining elevation, and the Prince informed them they were closing in on the source of the signal.

Breaking through the final curtain of vines, they emerged onto a rocky clearing. The Guardians sat back-to-back on a large rock. The pale, withered bodies of two large flying Grishki lay stacked to the side of a rectangular stone structure, engraved with worn writing and overgrown vegetation, that stood out amongst the organic rubble and jungle landscape.

Mari instantly recognized the writing, just like in her dreams, just like the cave back in Long Valley. She looked back at Greg and Jerro, making wide eyes. She had considered saying something. Sending something. A new thought crossed her mind. She wasn't sure now if Prince Lukyaza and the Guardians were capable of listening in. While she had been trusting them so far, her gut was telling her that something was off. Maybe it was nothing. She had heard the Prince's words. She was practicing restraint.

"This is not your work," the Prince said plainly, gesturing toward the insects as the Guardians stood and approached.

"No, their injuries are unique. They appear to have been drained. Life energy pulled from their bodies." Guardian Natal reported.

"Let us proceed on mission. Guardians, take up the rear. Mari, if you're feeling up to it, join me in the front. Jerro and Greg fill in between." The Prince ordered the group.

Mari made her way to the Prince. Phlip followed at her side now. As she stepped, her legs shook from the lingering effects of the toxin. A tingling sensation wrapped her skull. Another side effect or nerves? She shot a quick glance back at Jerro and Greg as they started moving towards the entrance. They knew what did this to the Grishki.

Hyrax.

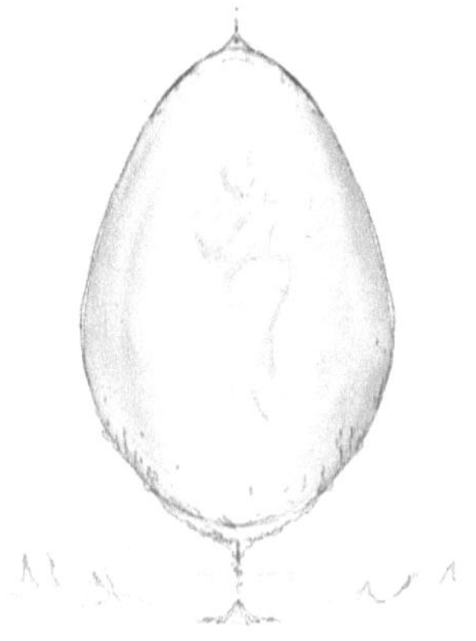

CHAPTER 12 | EGG

The column of rodentia led by the cloaked prince entered the cave through the chiseled rectangular archway. The engraved writing was similar, yet this cave was distinctly unique from the one Mari had awoken in back in Long Valley.

Daylight faded quickly as the formation progressed into the cave. Their eyes adapted. Pupils expanded to allow the faintest light to enter. Even in The Burrow, there was at least some ambient light from the bioluminescence. This was different. A deep darkness, an unnatural darkness.

The Guardians deployed the same autonomous drones that had patrolled the camp earlier. Their faint glow provided a brief reprieve from the utter darkness as they swept down the chiseled corridor, then returned and hovered in place.

Lukyaza passed a tiny disc to Mari, like the one he had used for translation. The Guardians did the same for Jerro and Greg.

"Place these on your temples." The Prince whispered.

They followed the order and were greeted with a mental heads-up display that cut through the dark. It did not just illuminate their vision. It organized it. A crisp overlay settled across the cave walls with thin brackets and clean lines.

Information crawled over the stone in small, steady readouts. Rock composition. Fracture patterns. Structural stability that updated as they shifted and breathed. Faint warnings pulsed near the ceiling where the stone looked sound to the naked eye.

A small picture in picture window opened in the corner of their sight, showing the drone's vision. The feed was stabilized and annotated with distance markers and motion pings, and a simple route line traced back toward them.

The Prince turned and continued down the hall, speaking in a hushed tone. "You are all now tapped into the psionic matrix transduction field. These devices interface with the psionic architecture that permeates the universe."

He slowed and looked back at them, letting the silence hang.

A clean confirmation pulse clicked through their minds, like a lock engaging.

His next words arrived without sound, plain and clipped, delivered with the flat precision of a system prompt. *Comms are live. Keep your thoughts tight.*

Mari's thoughts raced. *Was this network separate from Lunda's? Or layered on top of it? How did you even control what stayed private when thinking was the whole mechanism?* She held still and waited for a response from anyone. Her friends. Lunda. The Prince. The Guardians. None came.

This network felt different. Artificial instead of organic. Routed instead of shared. With Lunda, the psionosol frequency had felt communal, like stepping into the same room. This felt structured, more like you were plugged in, with hard edges and strict rules.

Mari reached for the familiar thread anyway, the one that had always been *theirs*, and pushed her thought down it like she was testing a door. *You two still with me?*

Yeah, Greg sent back at once. *You feel it too? This Borruki layer. Same space, different wiring.*

Jerro's reply came steadier. *Still us. Different channel.* A pause. *And… Lunda's gone. I shut down the core.*

Mari let the truth settle. *So we're on our own.*

They continued in a file, single and tight, farther into the network of tunnels.

A squelch followed by a resisted sucking sound broke the silence.

"Oh, gross!" Jerro blurted.

Natal's thought slammed down the line. *Silence.*

Jerro winced. *Sorry. Stepped in something. It's cold. It's… moving.*

Hold still, Lukyaza sent, already moving back toward him. *Let me see.*

A black, tarry substance coated Jerro's foot. It pulsed in a slow, wrong rhythm. He flipped down his sound-enhancing monocular and watched it reverberate at an odd frequency. A pattern emerged, like a waveform trying to become language. A group of *A* and *W* sounds.

A—wa—wa, Jerro sent, confused. *Awawa?*

Maxuun's reply was immediate. *Explain.*

Jerro swallowed. *I don't know. That's what it—*He frowned, focusing. *I think I can invert the frequency. Collapse the waveform.*

He pressed a paw to his temple and produced a barely audible tone. The tarry black ichor answered immediately, vibrating in clean, tight waves. He pushed the frequency higher. The mass constricted, cracked, and dropped away in granules from his webbed foot.

Interesting, Prince Lukyaza communicated calmly as the Guardians looked at him through their open visors.

They went deeper into the cave system. The tunnel here was crudely carved, a stark mismatch to the carefully etched entrance behind them. The tarry substance thickened as they went, spreading across the walls and ceiling until only a thin pathway remained underfoot. Step by step it narrowed, then vanished entirely—soon the whole way was covered in tarry muck.

With novel prudence, Mari was about to suggest they turn back when a faint red glow illuminated the tunnel ahead.

The Prince stopped in his tracks and threw up a quick, fisted paw. *Freeze.* The two drones zipped silently down the cavern toward the source of the light.

The display seamlessly integrated the drones' views, creating a layered, multidimensional space as it mapped the cave ahead. A soft green hexagonal pattern overlaid the real-world structures, illuminating edges and contours just beyond their natural sight.

As the drones moved deeper into the red glow, the foremost drone's feed suddenly went static and dropped off. In the second drone's footage, the first drone froze mid-flight. It slowly rotated toward the second drone, then accelerated at high speed toward it.

The collision sent a jolt of feedback through the heads-up display that drove the entire group to shudder. Their fur stood on end as the sensation tore through their minds. The overlay collapsed. A deep darkness consumed the space again, lit now only by the red glow emanating from around the corner.

Comms check, Lukyaza sent.

Up. Visuals down, Natal returned.

Jerro's personal display showed the same modulated frequency coming off the deep, seeping muck. The waveform pulsed, flowing toward the source of the light.

Jerro moved to the lead and turned back toward the others. *Stay close. I've got a path.* His confidence shook as he overrode the swelling fear.

He focused on the substance and inverted the frequency again, collapsing the waveform into a linear path. The tarry sludge subsided through the center of the cavern, and Jerro pushed forward, paw to his temple, guiding the group through the sticky mess.

As they approached the corner, the familiar wave of nausea swept through them. This feeling confirmed what they had already known. *This was certainly hyrax activity.*

The crude tunnel opened into a sharply contrasting chamber with expansive vaulted ceilings. Suspended in the center of the room was a large egg-shaped object, emanating its own sapphire hue that mixed with the scarlet glow. Together they formed a violet boundary that ebbed and flowed around it, as if the colors were locked in battle.

Within the egg was a silhouetted object, the details impossible to make out. The gooey substance coated the room completely, masking any architecture that might have existed beneath it.

Below the egg stood the monstrosity. Jerro instantly recognized the beast from Deepworks. The one who murdered Keeper

Aleese. Knowing what the creature was now made the scene somehow more disturbing than the first time. The behemoth hyrax stood on its hind legs, channeling a merged stream of energy that coalesced from the six smaller hyraxes positioned around it.

Before any of the group could act, the bottom of the egg cracked and shattered as fluid poured out. A furless, bipedal creature followed. Its limp body slapped onto the wet stone floor.

The tyrant looked over its shoulder at the group and let off a small sneer and, in its low throaty language, gave a quiet command.

The smaller hyrax turned, emitting a series of deep red blasts towards the group. Jerro summoned a shield that deflected the blasts, sending them careening around the cavernous chamber.

The Guardians ripped forward as their powered suits carried them through the air towards the formation of hyrax, their shoulder turrets deploying and returning a volley of their own. Of the barrage, only one blast contacted a hyrax, causing it to vibrate intensely and disintegrate into the sludge.

The hyrax leader snapped his head toward them, whiskers flaring, lips peeling back at the audacity of it. He raised a paw. A column of jet-black ichor shot from the opposing wall, ripping through both guardians, consuming them in darkness. When it pulled back into the wall, nothing remained.

Maxuun, Natal, report! The Prince commanded over comms. Silence was the response. Then a voice. The same gravelly words permeated their minds. *They have been consumed, and your fates will soon align.*

"NOOO!" The Prince roared aloud and shot into the air. "Lukyaza, don't!" Mari pleaded.

In a flash, the Prince channeled a massive blast. His arms gestured with precision as the room shook, broken stone and masses of tar fell from the ceiling.

They could feel the psionic energy—they could see it. Like it were a blanket that covered everything, a fabric that pulled inwards towards Lukyaza. He drew it in around him and through him.

The three friends huddled together as the room rocked violently. The power from the blast drew everything into it—sound, matter, even time itself seemed to slow. Jerro channeled his shield. Aided by Greg and Mari, he expanded it just wide enough to contain the three of them plus Phlip, who pressed his fluffy body close into the group.

Then it stopped, a calm returned and darkness resumed in the space. *Lukyaza?* Mari questioned over the Borruki net.

He did not answer. Rubble encapsulated them just outside of Jerro's barrier. Its faint yellow glow illuminated the rock as it settled in tightly.

Mari reached into her pack and grabbed out her lantern, expanding and twisting it to activate it. She snapped it onto Phlip's harness.

Jerro grit his teeth, eyes narrowing. He pushed out a struggled thought. *You see a way out?*

Greg was investigating the rock wall just beyond the shielding. "I'm not sure. There's a seam here. Drop the shield—just here."

Let me try. Jerro responded and shifted his weight toward Greg. He moved his free paw over and made a grasping motion, attempting to reduce the shield.

Rubble dropped through the area next to Greg. "That's it, just a little more!" He let off a thunderous paw strike that sent the rubble flying.

The crimson glow permeated the broken rubble.

Mari moved up next to Greg, trying to glimpse the scene. "Are they still out there?"

Greg started manually pushing some of the loose rock out of the way. "Must be." He hoisted himself through the small hole to poke his head out.

As he crested the rubble, he saw the large hyrax carrying the bipedal creature over its shoulder and dragging Prince Lukyaza by foot through a dark circular portal.

"Guys, we gotta go quick!" Greg said to them as he pulled his body through and reached a paw down for Mari.

She grabbed on and they pulled up Phlip behind her.

The red glow snapped out of existence. Mari's gentle blue lantern was now the only source of light.

"Jerro, when I say so, release the shield!" Greg said urgently.

He reached his paw back down into the void. "NOW!" Greg yelled.

Greg and Mari pulled Jerro out as the rubble collapsed inward, consuming the temporary refuge created by the shield.

The hyrax were gone, but the portal remained. Swirling with a deep oily darkness. Pearlescent hues reflected on the murmuring surface as it drew down. It was closing too fast.

Mari reflected on Rufus' brief lesson back on Station. Her body relaxed. Time slowed as each breath she took lengthened. The portal's closure halted. She had it—she stopped it.

Mari locked eyes with her friends and then Phlip. She had been brash. Her decisions had put them in danger. Here though, her inaction and restraint had been equally hazardous. *Decisions must be made.*

Mari swallowed. "No more waiting. We go for it."

They confidently waded into the portal. Following Mari. Following their instinct.

CHAPTER 13 | THE GLORP

Mari's body was the first to impact the oily surface. Terror consumed her mind. A wave of disorienting nausea followed, stronger than anything she had felt in her first encounter at Tailweavers. The oily substrate permeated her fur with a deep cold that pierced into her core. Darkness swallowed her vision, followed by a barely audible sound that rose sharply into something like a popping sensation. It almost sounded like it said… *glorp*?

As she stepped into this realm, the ground was less sticky than she expected. The landscape was made of fine black rock, smooth as glass, stretching outward in gentle slopes and hard angles. A crackle of red energy flashed through the sky, blotted with deep gray, jagged clouds. Each burst of light refracted through the black surface below, throwing brief colors across the ground. The brighter ones faded quickly, as if being pulled down into the rock by gravity.

Jerro, Greg, and Phlip emerged through the portal behind her. To her surprise, they were not coated in tar the way she had imagined they might be after what happened in the cave.

Greg surveyed the strange horizon. "Where in the burrow are we?" he asked aloud, his voice echoing off the rock.

"No idea." Mari replied, scanning the open space for any sign of the hyrax.

Jerro's nose wrinkled. He sniffed the air in quick succession. "Oh, man… do you smell that?"

"No wha–" Mari started, but she was interrupted by her own gag reflex and had to swallow back bile.

A sickly-sweet, rotten stink of putrid fruit overtook the group. Mari turned toward her friends just as the portal snapped closed behind them. Their tracking bracelets from Station flipped to a red glow, then faded out, severing their link to the system. Where the portal had been, something else remained.

An amorphous blob of malformed flesh stood in its place, re-shaping itself in slow, wet movements. An eye opened where no eye should be. A mouth formed lower down, drooling saliva that stringed and snapped as it fell. *How did we miss this?* Mari thought. *It must have been obscured by the portal.*

The creature coughed up what looked like a cracked egg from its mouth, then let out a small yet deep, ferociously distorted roar. It expanded in size like it was being inflated, and the flesh rolled outward in thick layers toward Phlip.

Phlip's glassy eyes expanded to full size. He tried to hop away, but a slab of meat slammed down in his path, blocking him like a wall.

"Phlip!" Mari yelled in horror. In unison, the friends rallied to his aid.

Jerro dropped his monocular down over one eye, searching for anything that could give them an opening. Greg and Mari moved in a choreographed sequence that felt familiar, like their engagement with the giant earthworm had trained their bodies more than they realized.

Greg began a rotational gesture. It was intuitive, yet completely novel, like his paws were following instructions written into the air. Mari charged toward him, sliding down a smooth section of black rock that offered almost no resistance. The surface was slick, but predictable, and she used it to build speed. As she reached Greg, she leapt, and his rotation guided her into orbit around him.

Words became unnecessary. They were one. Senses, minds, ability, all melded into a single timing. Mari's rotation accelerated, her fur and outline beginning to glow a deep shade of blue. As she spun, her body assumed geometric forms that seemed to bend what they knew of reality. Cubes, spheres, diamonds, appearing in brief impressions that flickered and then smoothed back into her shape.

Jerro saw something through the monocular. Just like the pipe in Deepworks, there was an unusual vibration hidden in the rock. A subtle shimmer, almost like heat distortion, but localized to a specific outcropping. *Obsidian.* He recognized it from his geology studies from Builders Basic, the way it held tension and how it failed when pushed the right way.

He placed a paw to his temple and focused his frequency modulation on the outcropping. If he could fracture it cleanly, a sharp slab of obsidian could be sheared off. Not dust—not rubble—a single edge.

Mari built speed until her orbit tightened. Her posture changed, not tense, but purposeful. Hind paws dangling gently together, arms stretched loosely to her sides, her orientation fixed on the creature engulfing Phlip.

This all happened in mere seconds.

The rock face sheared as Jerro had anticipated. The obsidian split with a crisp break that felt too clean for a place like this. Mari launched from the rotation, tearing toward the flesh mass with tremendous speed. Greg and Jerro both raised their paws to shield their eyes as the ambient light seemed to pull inward toward Mari's glow.

Mari tore through the creature almost instantly, carving a gaping chasm through the mass of flesh. Simultaneously, the razor-sharp slab of obsidian was drawn into her path as the local psionic structure faltered. The supporting field that held the creature's shape and orientation stuttered, and gravity behaved differently in that narrow corridor.

That was enough.

The slab snapped into the wake of Mari's passage and cut through what remained, rendering the creature into pieces that flew off with the obsidian into the distance, tumbling across the black rock until the red light swallowed them.

Mari stood at a distance, facing the group, panting, the blue glow fading back into the dimness.

Phlip dropped a few pellets onto the black rock and hopped over toward Greg and Jerro, seemingly unaffected by the entire event.

That was… unreal, Jerro sent, *lungs burning.*

Mari was already sprinting back. Phlip bounced to meet her, exuberant as ever.

"Now, let's go find this giant creep!" Mari said when she reached them.

Jerro shrugged off his pack. "Hey. I've got something that might help."

He pulled out his Decanter of Aquarius. "No, that's not it," he said, then paused. "But I am thirsty…" He took a swig from the container and swapped it for another item. "Ah, this is it." He produced a worn map case, unlatched it, and slid the parchment out in a slow roll, flattening it as it emerged.

The map shimmered into view and wavered—more suggestion than chart. Lines and circles, odd shapes looping and branching, as if it were identifying relationships instead of landmarks.

"Hmmm… That's not very helpful," Jerro muttered, giving it a frustrated shake.

"That crazy thing from Rufus's study… How is that going to help us?" Greg asked. It was the same question Mari would have asked, but she was still cooling down from the recent event, her breathing only just returning to normal.

"I thought… I thought maybe we could make sense of it," Jerro said. "I'd sort of forgotten about it until just now, but maybe it can help us track them down. Rufus must have wanted us to take it for a reason."

They leaned in as the map reorganized itself. The oily ink shifted in slow waves, dragging against their paws like static. A local landscape revealed, fading at the edges as if it refused to commit beyond a certain distance. Along the top, words appeared in a language they understood—formed from their thoughts more than the page.

The Glorp.

"That's the sound from the portal!" Mari said, pointing at the title. "Must be what this place is called?"

Jerro stared at it, then glanced back at the strange horizon. "Maybe." He said, half to himself.

"Look over there." Mari added, pointing into the distance at a spire-like structure. She looked back down at the map. "That must be this place." Her paw traced a similar shape that was drawing itself out in the ink like the parchment was catching up to what she was seeing.

"It seems like the most logical place to start." Jerro agreed.

They took off in a file toward the spire. Mari led the group, mounted on Phlip's back, Jerro followed in the middle, gliding on his disk, and Greg took up the rear on all fours, making quick work of the challenging terrain. They navigated the unsettling planescape carefully, weaving between massive outcroppings of jagged stone and doing their best to hold a linear path in their chosen direction.

Despite moving toward the spire, it seemed to move as well. Mari was sure of it. She distinctly remembered the mountain behind the spire that looked like a large cookie with a bite taken out of it. That formation was now far down the horizon, too far for it to be explained by their movement alone.

"Guys," Jerro said, and his voice tightened. "I'm picking up something on my monocular. I think it's tracks. Not footprints, but psionic essence." He paused, searching for a description that he had no words for. "I've got two powerful signatures, and a third one that's… unique. It's not psionic. It's anomalous. I've never seen any-thing quite like it. The psionic matrix seems to be warping along the path."

"Whatever it is, we face it together." Mari responded. Greg gave a firm nod of commitment.

The terrain shifted ahead of them. Beyond a razor ridge of ob-sidian, a plain of dark blue grass stretched out toward the spire, which was now fully visible from base to precipice. The field was dotted with pools of dark, tarry liquid, the same substance Jerro had stepped in back in the tunnels. Singular flesh monsters wandered through the open spaces. Some climbed in and out of the ichor pools. Others sat motionless, as though they were waiting. A few grew and transformed in place, rearranging themselves into various configura-tions as though they were testing different shapes.

Then the wind shifted.

A blast of rotten banana aroma rolled across the field, thick enough to taste, drawn toward them like a warning.

They lined up along the ridge crest. Lying flat, their bodies pressed tightly against the stone to avoid giving away their location. Together they took in the scene.

"I'm assuming we will want to avoid that?" Greg whispered.

"Look," Mari whispered, pointing toward the spire. "It is moving. I knew it."

The spire was crawling along, supported by a mass of rolling tar that carried it forward and left a wake of residue behind. Up close, it was not just one tower, but a complex of helical spires coalescing into a single structure that reached into the blood-red sky. Beyond it, a distant mountain chain sat in silhouette, rugged against the clouds.

"Okay," Mari said, keeping her voice low as she tracked its movement. "Look at the path it's taking. It's heading toward that stretch where the ridge tapers down into the field." She gestured with her paw to outline the angle. "If we hurry, I think we can beat it there. It's not moving that fast. Then we just have to figure out how to get on it."

Greg held out a fisted paw toward the center of the group. Mari and Jerro placed their paws in.

Jerro cleared his throat, dead serious. "Pawple Horizon." He waited for approval with a hopeful smile. "You know, like purple, but I changed the 'pur' to 'paw'."

Mari blinked. "Jerro. What—why are you like this?"

"The ship name," Greg said, like this was normal. "He's trying to come up with names for the ship." He kept his tone calm. "Jerro, that's a great name. Let's keep exploring our options. Assuming we make it out of here."

Jerro lit up. "I get it. Maybe that isn't the one. But the name is in here somewhere." He tapped his skull with a grin.

"Let's get moving," Mari said, pulling them back on track. She hopped up and slung herself onto Phlip. "Come on."

They slipped down the back side of the ridge toward the interception point she had picked.

They beat the spire there, but it was moving quicker than Mari had anticipated. In moments it would pass their position, close enough to count details. Fifty tails or fewer.

The ground trembled as the fortress sloughed forward, carried by the rolling tar mass beneath it. A flesh creature wandered too close, and the tar rolled over it. It disappeared entirely, consumed without a struggle, leaving only a smear that blended back into the undulating mass.

Mari stared up at the structure as it neared. There was no clear path up. The fortress was nearly as high as it was far away.

Shadows flickered over their hiding place. All four of them looked up together.

Half a dozen large flying creatures landed on a balcony perched high on the spire, folding their wings as if the tower belonged to them.

"No way I can make that jump," Greg said, eyeing the height and distance.

"Maybe not," Jerro replied, scanning through his monocular. His voice stayed calm, but his focus sharpened. "But maybe there's another way." He angled the monocular toward the rear of the moving fortress. "Check that out."

A small hatch opened. Three hyraxes emerged carrying long pitchforks. They jabbed down into the rolling tar and worked their tools with practiced rhythm, extracting bits and pieces of the flesh creature that had been swallowed moments earlier. They lifted the pieces out like harvest, inspecting them briefly before dragging them back toward the hatch.

Greg watched, then grimaced. "Uhh... I totally get what you're thinking, Jerro, but look at that thing. It's been dismembered."

The window to act was closing quickly as the spire approached the tapered outcropping and began to align with Mari's chosen point.

"Trust me, guys. On my tail," Jerro said, instinct taking over. He floated out from the rocks on his disk, moving toward the front edge of the tar mass.

Mari and Greg looked at each other. With an exasperated shrug, they followed.

Jerro pushed the thought to them as they ran. *I'm not sure what kind of forces we're going to have to withstand, so I will need both of you.* He glanced back once, then pointed to the ground. *Gather here fast, and channel everything you've got into me.*

They formed a small triangle with Phlip in the middle and Jerro facing the approaching fortress, his back to them.

Jerro took a knee in concentration, head down, paw pressed to his temple. The rolling tar mass drew closer. The rocks trembled beneath them, and dust kicked up in small bursts with each heavy slide of the spire's movement.

Jerro looked up quickly and stood.

A sphere of crackling energy erupted around them, then stabilized, spreading thin tendrils between them like taut lines. Jerro turned fully toward the oncoming mass and braced for impact.

It consumed them entirely with the same *glorp* sound they had heard at the portal. It was dark, dimly lit only by the deep yellow glow of Jerro's protective barrier. Their location, direction of travel, and orientation were quickly lost as the tar blotted out all external reference.

Mari and Greg strained, driving their energy into Jerro to maintain the shield.

The forces are intense. Jerro sent, his thoughts tight and measured, *but if we can maintain this for a few more moments, we should be okay. I timed how long it took for the flesh monster. We only have to hold it for four minutes.*

Four minutes, while brief, felt like four hours to the friends as they fought with every molecule of their being to keep the barrier intact. It fluctuated more than once, and Jerro rearranged the structure to support the shifting load. Chunks of flesh, rock, and other debris crashed into the field, changing the pressure and strain in unpredictable bursts.

We're almost there! Mari sent, and clung to it.

She didn't know that, not truly, but she felt it. Or she needed to. She imagined that if she could will it into existence for herself, it could be true for all of them.

They were almost there.

A fork pierced the force field, and tar began leaking in. Phlip shifted slightly to avoid the spilling goo and scratched his ear, calm in a way that reflected his ignorance of the danger. Mari almost laughed, then caught it in her throat. This was not the time, but Phlip was still Phlip.

Light poured in through the breach and quickly spread around the sphere, illuminating the scene beyond the barrier.

Greg, hit them quick. I can hold this with Jerro! Mari sent urgently.

Greg shot up through the hole as Jerro widened it, forcing the hyrax's fork to come free.

The gang of hyraxes stood on a platform just above the rolling tar foundation, completely unprepared for what came next. In one sweeping, practiced movement, Greg launched himself forward, and it looked for a moment like he was running on open air just above their position. He moved with blinding speed, his path precise and controlled.

His first impact alone knocked one hyrax off the platform into the gooey foundation below. It disappeared immediately, swallowed without a trace.

Greg was already on the next one. His movement became so fast it was hard to follow, as if he was phasing from one position to the other. He drove an Earthshaker Pawstrike into its sternum.

The hyrax's body barely shifted, but something else did.

Its ephemeral essence tore backward into space and dissipated into the red sky. The physical form seemed to lose cohesion, bonds releasing at an atomic level, and collapsed into a pile of unidentifiable particulate.

The third hyrax turned and fled toward a large service door. It reached for the control panel.

It wasn't quick enough. Greg was already there, behind it.

He pivoted and drove a rounded kick through its side. The impact landed with a dull, unreal heaviness, and the air rippled with psionic pressure. The hyrax skidded across the deck, slammed into a railing, and went limp in a crumpled heap.

Greg grabbed one of the forks and ran to the edge of the platform where the shielded sphere was sinking back into the tar.

"Grab on!" he shouted, lowering the fork down toward the barrier.

Mari reached up with one paw, splitting her focus to catch the end of the pitchfork while still feeding energy into Jerro. The shield shuddered. Jerro strained. The tar pressed and pulled around them like a living weight.

As they rose from the muck, Jerro could let the upper portion of the barrier down, thinning it until it became less of a sphere and more of a protective bowl around their bodies.

With all their might, Greg, Mari, Jerro and Phlip pulled themselves free of the deadly foundation.

They collapsed onto the deck, breathing hard, tar spattering their fur. Above them, the sky shifted to a deeper shade of red and bruise-dark orange.

226

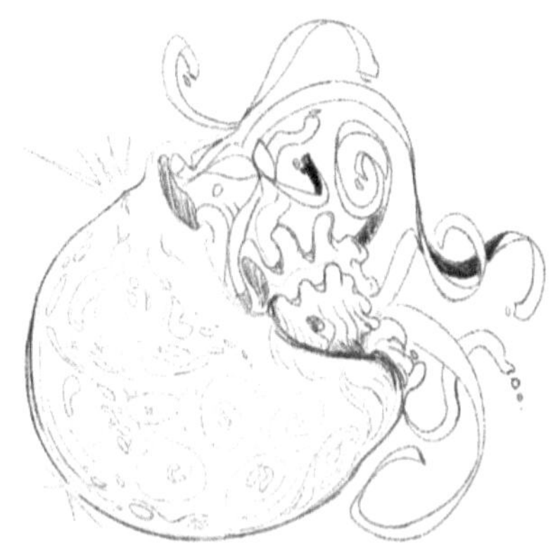

CHAPTER 14 | INTERLUDE

With their backs pressed against the cold metal surface of the articulating platform, the three friends and Phlip took a moment to gather themselves. Phlip lay nuzzled against Mari, his large floppy head resting over her shoulder, breathing slow and steady as if none of what had just happened could possibly apply to him.

Above them, an array of glowing orbs dotted the sky, floating in from the distant mountain range. As they drew closer, long tendrils came into view, trailing beneath the spectral lavender spheres like roots in still water. The red sky behind them was still heavy with jagged clouds, but here, for the first time since entering The Glorp, the world felt like it had paused.

Mari pulled out some pizza and, without a word, distributed a slice to her exhausted friends. The act was simple, almost normal, and for a moment that made it feel more real than anything else around them. With the spire still high in their field of view, they all knew there was more work ahead, but no one spoke it.

One of the floating orbs detached from the formation and drifted closer to the platform. Within the mass of glowing jelly, what looked like a miniature universe coalesced, swimming with stars and galaxies. Colors swirled inside it with a quiet purpose as the tendrils lowered until they hovered within a tail's length.

Mari felt calm wash over her, like the weight of The Glorp had been lifted. The nausea in her chest softened. The tightness in her shoulders loosened. A voice spoke into her mind, steady and soothing.

Even in darkness, there is light. In pain, relief. In despair, hope.

The tips of the tendrils loosened and flaked down toward them, like massive snowflakes on a calm winter day. The group basked in the brief respite as a surge of energy moved through their bodies, subtle at first, then stronger. It did not feel like the sharp, hungry kind of power Mari had used in battle. This was quieter. It seeped in like warmth through frigid fur.

The jelly tips glowed intensely upon landing. Mari picked one up to examine it in her small paw. The calm was overwhelming, and with it came an urge to consume the jelly, to accept whatever it offered without question.

That was the old Mari. The version of herself that dove head-first into every unknown because stopping felt like weakness.

She held the jelly tip between her claws and forced herself to breathe. She looked at Greg, at Jerro, at Phlip still leaning against her like the world was safe. The spire hung above them, patient and waiting, as though it knew time always moved forward again.

Choices still had to be made.

Mari brought the jelly to her mouth.

The texture was smooth and firm with a mildly honeyed, clean taste. A wave of energy pulsed through her mind in a faded reverberation—not violent, not forcing, but undeniable. She fell back, but did not hit the metal. Instead, she floated gently, just above the platform, as if the air had decided to hold her.

Jerro and Greg watched as Mari's eyes flashed to a soft white glow, faint hues of blue streaking outward. Her arms and legs rested loosely, balanced in a posture that was neither tense nor limp. For the first time in a long time, she looked like she was allowing herself to be carried.

∞

Mari was back in the temple from her dream.

Ornate white columns rose around her, and the segmented mosaic map covered the floor. It felt familiar now, but not comforting. Familiar in the way a pattern is familiar when you can't stop seeing it.

What is this place? She thought again. *Why do I keep coming here?*

She walked across the mosaic, slower than she used to, taking in the shape of it rather than rushing to the edge where she had searched for waiting answers. The map was not static. Pieces of it shifted subtly as she moved, responding to her presence. She could sense paths forming and dissolving, like the temple wanted her to understand that direction was not something you found. It was something you chose.

She reached the outer edge, where steps led down into a cracked clay landscape. The ground stretched until it disappeared into a line of silhouetted mountains reaching up toward a dark, blood-red sky.

The sky was familiar.

This was The Glorp.

For a moment she stood on the top step and watched the horizon. She could feel the pull within herself, the instinct to leap forward, to chase the next thing simply because it was there. She could also feel a different truth settling beneath that instinct. Restraint was not fear. Balance was not hesitation. It was knowing that every choice created a path, and some paths could not be undone once you stepped onto them.

The red sky flickered with distant light, and Mari realized that the temple was not asking her to stop moving.

It was asking her to move with intention.

The world shifted.

∞

The same red sky, dotted with glowing orbs, filled her vision again as her eyes returned to normal. Her body settled back against the smooth metal of the platform, the spire still looming above her. Her chest rose and fell slowly. She felt steadier, something in her aligned rather than altered.

A second jelly flake drifted down and landed near Jerro's paw. It pulsed once, faint and patient, like it was waiting for a decision.

Jerro stared at it. His instincts told him to catalog it, not consume it, but Mari was back now, and Greg's eyes were fixed on the sky in the way they got when he was trying not to feel something. Jerro lifted the jelly tip and ate it, slow and deliberate, as though control could be measured in small choices.

Warmth spread behind his eyes. His monocular flickered on its own, then steadied. The platform, the spire, and the red sky softened at the edges.

∞

He was standing in a space that felt thin, like reality had been pressed into a single layer.

The ground beneath his feet was dark and glossy, not quite stone, not quite liquid. It shifted in slow segments, panels sliding and settling as if the surface was deciding what shape it wanted to be. Oily ink threaded through the seams in quiet currents. Above him, faint lines of light crossed the air in careful spans and triangles, reorganizing into load paths as he looked at them. It reminded him of stress diagrams and tunnel bracing, except the material here was thought and motion, not rock.

Jerro lifted a paw, and the lattice responded—not bending—not breaking. Reconfiguring in quiet obedience.

A presence formed beside him. Not a body. Not a voice at first. More like a familiar alignment in his thoughts, a pattern he recognized the way he recognized his own name.

Lunda.

Her presence did not arrive as sound. It arrived as clarity. A gentle correction. A calm pulse that made his mind feel less alone.

You're still trying to hold everything yourself, she sent. There was no judgment in it. Only recognition.

Jerro swallowed. *You're... here?*

Not fully. Not like before, Lunda replied. *But you are on a layer where echoes can persist. Where structure can be remembered.*

The space around him reorganized. Beneath his feet, the glossy panels slid and settled, seams darkening as boundaries and features emerged, a larger pattern finally snapping into focus. Farther out, the landscape faded at the edges, refusing to commit beyond a certain distance.

A path traced itself across the surface. A slow, crawling line that matched the spire's movement. Under it, dark currents flowed like rivers.

And within those flows was a unique energy.

It did not fit with the others in this place. Not psionic, yet it influenced the psionic architecture around it. Wherever it moved, the surface warped slightly, like reality itself was being asked to bend.

Jerro focused on the warped signature. The lattice trembled, a subtle warning rippling through the space.

Careful, Lunda sent. *That anomaly isn't noise. It's a rule being rewritten.*

Jerro's builder mind latched onto the idea immediately. *So, it's not just something we're chasing. It's changing the ground we're standing on.*

Yes, Lunda said, and the lattice shifted into a tighter pattern, like a brace being installed. *You will have to understand its constraints.*

Jerro tried to hold the pattern steady in his mind. The crawling path. The tar rivers. The warped signature. He tried to store it like a drawing before it faded.

The lines of light dimmed. The segmented panels slowed. Lunda's presence softened, like she was stepping backward into fog.

Jerro, she said, and the smallest note of warmth threaded into her calm. *You are not alone.*

∞

Then he was back on the articulating platform, blinking at the red sky. He slowly shifted his gaze from Greg to Mari and finally to Phlip. Jerro's breathing was steady, but his eyes looked farther than the spire now, as if he could still see the pattern beneath everything.

A third jelly flake drifted down and landed near Greg's foot. He stared at it for a long moment, like the decision mattered more than the substance itself.

He thought of his trial. The moment his body hesitated when it should not have. The way the others had looked at him afterward. He never even told his father, but he imagined his face had gone still. Not angry—not loud. Just finished. Disappointed in a way that did not need words.

Greg ate the jelly tip in one motion before he could change his mind.

∞

The world did not go dark. It went quiet.

Greg stood on black glass rock, clean and untouched by tar, and the red sky above was softer here, the storm withdrawn just enough to give him room. Ahead, the ground ended. A chasm separated him from a suspended platform. He stepped out with a paw, nothing waiting beneath. It was the same vulnerable feeling he'd found during the fight, that brief certainty that his next step wouldn't exist the moment he placed it.

He moved anyway, taking one step. Then another.

Each stone formed beneath him at the last moment, like his very movement created it. It felt like freedom, and that scared him more than the monsters ever did.

A figure waited ahead on the path. Not a full body at first. A silhouette sharpened in the red light. Broad shoulders. Familiar posture. A presence that carried weight.

His father.

Greg stopped. His chest tightened. He could feel the old reflex rise up—the one that kept his emotions contained, the one that made him stand straight and accept whatever verdict came next.

His father did not speak right away. He just looked at Greg the way he always had, as though Greg had become a problem to solve.

Then the voice came into his mind, not gentle, not cruel. Simply true, in the way a rule is true.

You were supposed to be steady.

Greg's throat tightened. He tried to speak, but nothing came out, like the dream was forcing him to stay in the place he always stayed. Silent and controlled. Trapped in his own composure.

He took a breath and pushed words into the space anyway. *I was steady,* and even as he sent it, he felt how defensive it sounded. *I just… I hesitated.*

Hesitation is failure, his father replied.

Greg felt heat rise behind his eyes. He hated that the words still worked on him, even here. He hated that the lineage lived inside his bones like gravity.

The stepping stones beneath his feet shook. For a moment he thought the path was going to collapse and drop him into the red sky.

Then another presence appeared.

Not his father's weight. Something lighter. Something that did not demand. It arrived as a simple thought, almost like Mari's voice when she believed in him without trying to fix him.

You are allowed to choose, the presence shared.

Greg turned, searching for it. There was no figure, no face. Just the feeling of permission.

His father stepped forward, and the pressure returned. "You are a product of our line. You don't get to choose. You uphold."

Greg's body trembled. He realized he had been holding his breath.

"I don't want to be a product," he said, and the thought surprised him with its steadiness. "I don't want to carry your disappointment like it's my name."

His father's expression did not change. That was the hardest part. No anger to fight. No softness to lean into. Just the expectation.

Greg looked down at his own paws. He remembered the Earthshaker Pawstrike. How precise it had been when he stopped thinking about proving anything. How clean it felt when he moved for his friends, not for approval.

He took a step forward.

The stepping stone formed beneath him, solid and certain.

His father did not move aside. Greg walked anyway, not through him, not past him, but toward the part of himself that had been trapped behind that expectation for so long.

He felt the pressure lessen.

Not vanish. Not heal all at once. But loosen, like a knot finally softening.

∞

Greg's vision filled with the looming spire. He was sitting with his back against the cold metal again. The pizza slice had gone limp in his paw. He stared at it for a moment, then took a slow bite, more out of habit than hunger.

His thoughts felt quieter now. Not empty. Just less crowded by someone else.

Above them, the iridescent swarm of orbs continued their slow drift across the red sky. The tendrils swayed gently, distant again, as though their brief offering had been all they intended.

Phlip shifted and sighed against Mari's shoulder. Jerro glanced between his friends, confirming they were still here. Still together.

The spire remained above them, patient and looming.

This reset was over.

And the choices ahead were theirs to make.

CHAPTER 15 | SUBTERFUGE

A plume of dark smoke billowed out from the front of the spire's foundation, followed by a grinding groan. The entire structure lurched and shuddered, slowing to a halt.

Jerro sat up abruptly. "You think they know?"

"Let's not wait around to find out," Mari said, and led the way through the large dark metallic doorway.

The interior was beyond dark, like the cave. The only exception was a faint red light that illuminated a narrow path ahead. It flowed in segmented lines down a winding corridor and terminated at a short set of stairs. As the light moved, its trail vanished instantly into the surrounding blackness, pulled under like blood into thirsty soil.

They started up the stairs cautiously.

Greg stumbled on the second step and caught himself against the wall. *I miss those drones,* he sent, irritation sharp in the link. *This place eats the light.*

Mari slowed, turning back. The red glow flickered across her helmet, then dimmed again, as though it noticed her noticing it.

What if we don't need drones, she sent. *Not exactly. What if we can do it? On purpose.* Mari hesitated on a step. *We keep finding new things when we're cornered. Maybe we're cornering ourselves.*

Jerro felt a brief tightening in his chest as her thought brushed against his, closer than usual. He was about to respond when Mari let her awareness slip outward.

She did not push. She reached.

It felt less like opening a door and more like extending a paw into cold water, unsure how deep it went. The sensation spread unevenly, thin at first, then widening as it moved beyond her body. Almost immediately she felt resistance, not from the space itself, but from the bonds already there.

Greg and Jerro. When Mari's awareness expanded, it caught on them like fabric on a hook. Before she could adjust, they were pulled with her.

Jerro's stomach lurched.

Too much information rushed in at once, overlapping impressions stacking without order. He instinctively searched for patterns, for edges and seams, and found them everywhere. The walls were not smooth. They carried shallow ridges and softened seams, like stone that had once been pliable and had hardened in layers. Reinforced sections rose in gentle arcs that did not match the geometry of the corridor, and stress lines spidered through the structure like veins under skin.

Okay, he sent, breath unsteady. *That's a lot. I'm getting structure. Too much structure.*

Greg barely noticed the walls. What caught him was movement. Not shapes or bodies, but intention. Subtle displacements in the air ahead. Pressure changes. The absence of stillness. His focus locked forward without him deciding to, instincts snapping into place as if this was something he had always known how to do.

Something is coming, Greg sent. *Not here yet, but moving toward us.*

Mari tightened her focus, instinctively pulling the shared awareness closer, compressing it until the noise dulled. The space sharpened in response. Not brighter, but clearer. Materials resolved themselves by feel rather than sight. Metal hummed faintly. Stone carried memory. Even the air had texture.

This was not a display or borrowed vision. It was messy and overwhelming and entirely theirs.

At the top of the stairs, the red lighting ended at an arched metal door. Mari placed a paw against it and extended just enough awareness to check beyond.

This room is clear, Mari sent.

She nodded, and they moved through together.

Inside, a block of metal with concave sides rested against one wall, clearly repurposed as a table. Spare pitchforks were mounted nearby. Hexagonal cards sat stacked in the center, flanked by three uneven piles. The air carried a sour foundation, topped with a sulfuric bite that stung their noses and caught in their throats. Across the room, a hatch stood open. A heap of flesh monster remains had been stacked beside it.

Jerro crouched and flipped the lid back, his focus narrowing. The information came through more cleanly this time. The hatch led to a chute, angled downward and reinforced for repeated use.

Before he could relay more, the shared awareness brushed outward again, unbidden this time.

They felt them.

Eight distinct presences moving through the adjoining hall. Coordinated. Armored. Close enough now that the air itself seemed to tense around the thought.

I'm not going down that hatch, Greg sent. The idea swam out before he could stop it.

No, Mari replied. *I have another plan. Follow my lead.*

The hyrax contingent burst into the room, cutting a direct path toward them.

Mari felt their psionosense falter all at once, not fading so much as collapsing under sudden pressure. The shared awareness they had been leaning on slipped away, like a thought pulled from their grasp just as it was forming. It was not gone entirely, but it was muted, compressed beneath something heavier that had entered the space with the hyrax.

The room lit in a neutral amber glow from a line of wall sconces set into the stone. Their light was steady and unbothered. A string of squeaks and guttural sounds came from the apparent leader as it stepped forward. Bold white lettering was emblazoned across its breastplate.

I-R-S.

Each hyrax carried a rugged blaster with elongated, rigid geometry held at the low ready. Their polearms remained sheathed along their backs.

They were not aiming at the friends, but they were close enough that Mari could feel the intent behind the formation. Ready, watching, waiting to be told otherwise.

Mari glanced back over her shoulder and gave a quick wink to Jerro and Greg, then turned to face the hyrax and answered with her own burst of choked squeaks and strained, uneven screams.

The sounds felt wrong as they left her mouth, but she did not try to correct them. Instead, she focused on the idea beneath the noise, forcing her intent to sit where meaning should have been. It took effort to hold, like keeping a shape from collapsing once the support was removed. Pressure thickened behind her eyes as she sustained it, and she became acutely aware of how fragile the illusion was.

Jerro and Greg exchanged a look, then both glanced down at Phlip, who was still chewing contentedly on a length of exposed wire, blissfully unaware of the tension filling the room.

A quick exchange of chirps and barks passed between the lead hyrax and another, then he turned and snapped commands to the rest. The formation shifted. Tension didn't vanish, but it loosened into something closer to indifference—whatever Mari had made them perceive was no longer worth immediate concern.

Half of the contingent filed out.

Mari shot a quick glance back at her friends and tugged Phlip in behind her as she started down the hall. She could feel the illusion thinning behind her, like fabric stretched too far. Jerro and Greg followed without hesitation. The remaining hyrax fell in around them, one ahead and two behind, closing them into a moving pocket as they advanced.

When did you learn to speak their language? Jerro asked. *And what did you say to them?*

I do not think I am, Mari replied, keeping her focus forward. *I was thinking about a lesson where we had to disguise a carrot. Make it look like something else. I could not do it then, but I thought maybe I could use the same technique on my words instead of an object.*

Well, what did you tell them? Greg asked. *Why do they trust us?*

I told them we pulled him out of the tar, Mari answered, flicking a glance between them and Phlip. *Made us look like hyraxes to them. I think they bought it, but I don't think I can do this again. Not like that.*

They continued down the corridor.

Now we have to take Phlip down to some containment area, Mari added. *Jerro, if you get a chance to break away, see what that magic map of yours is showing us in here. I'll tell them you have to go to the bathroom.*

I don't have to, Jerro replied immediately. *I'm good.*

No Jerro. I know. That is just so you can look at the map.

Oh... He nodded along with the thought. *Right.*

The halls were tight and took strange, organic paths, like they had been grown rather than built—layer upon layer, old and new pressed together, compacted into shape. As they climbed, Mari became aware of the spire itself in a way she could not fully explain. It was not watching them, exactly, but it was registering them. Whenever she leaned too hard on her psionics, the sensation brushed along the edges of her mind, slow and structural, like weight shifting deep within the foundation.

They wound up a staircase and passed a barred window.

Jerro slowed just long enough to peer out. *Halfway up, I'd esti-mate,* he sent.

Mari's foot slipped on the next step. Her focus wavered for only a moment, but the pressure surged in response. She stumbled forward before she could correct herself.

Greg caught her by the arm and steadied her without breaking stride.

How long do you think you can hold this? He asked, not accu-satory, just careful.

Her strain bled into the mindspace before she could pull it back. *I'm not sure,* Mari admitted. *It feels like something is building. Like the spire knows we don't belong here.*

She straightened and kept walking, forcing her breathing to slow.

Whatever was listening had not acted yet, but that did not mean it would wait.

As they marched along, they passed barracks, mechanical rooms, storage areas, kitchens, and open spaces full of hyrax running drills. Horrifying calls met them, a hard clattering that drove through the corridor and into their ribs. It came from ahead, from a wide hangar bay where the sound bounced and multiplied. This must have been where they had seen the birds land earlier.

The air carried damp straw and sharp bird musk, tightening their throats. Now close up, they could make out the details. The birds had robust frames coated in salted gray plumage. Yellow orbs sat high in their eye sockets. Their thick rounded bills clattered together as they called, the discordant drumming rolling out through the open bay door and into the abyss of The Glorp.

Through a door adjacent to the hangar, was a long hall lined with half a dozen cells on each side. Some had energized barriers up, enclosing the cell.

As they passed the first, a small mushroom with a swirling purple cap and white spots sat idly in the middle of the room.

The cell next to it was where the hyrax leader guided Mari and Phlip. As Mari settled Phlip into the cell, pretending he was an aggressive monster, Greg was drawn back to the mushroom. He took a step toward the yellow sheet of translucent energy that closed the cell.

Suddenly the mushroom opened one singular eye and pierced an intense stare through Greg. A white cloud of spores rushed out from under the cap and through the energy screen.

When it cleared, the mushroom was gone.

Greg touched his cheek. A fine powder spread smoothly between his paw pads.

Uh… Jerro, did you see that? Greg sent, while Mari continued her wrangling act with Phlip.

Jerro's eyes narrowed, and his head tilted. *See what?*

Greg looked at his paw. The spore dust had vanished.

In the cell, there was a little purple and white mushroom.

"That mushroom?" Jerro pointed back at the cell where Greg had looked away. "Yeah. What in the burrow…"

Mari yelled, herding Phlip the way you would a wild beast. "YAAA. YAAA." She danced around him, pretending to avoid his ferocious attacks. He playfully lunged and avoided her advances.

Finally, she wrestled him down. While it wasn't obvious to the hyrax, Phlip had let her. Greg and Jerro noticed, though, especially when she leaned close and whispered something in his ear that made him settle.

Mari stepped out of the cell confidently and gave a quick "Awawa!" and a salute to the hyrax leader. She had been studying their behavior while moving through the halls, and it was becoming convincing.

The guard slapped the control panel next to the cell, and the sheet of yellow energy enclosed Phlip.

Phlip looked at Mari with his confused glassy eyes. He attempted to follow, to push through the barrier, but it stopped him with a shock that sent him leaping back. In the far corner, he curled into a ball, ears tucked flat, face buried.

Mari fought back her emotions and regained her composure. She had a job to do.

The lead hyrax took them out of the containment area and exchanged some grunts and screeches with Mari.

Mari suppressed her emotions and sent a quick message, convenient as the knot in her throat would have prevented much actual speech. *Alright guys, I think he's gonna leave us to 'get back on our own'.*

Jerro's eyes relaxed. *Whew. I'm just glad we don't have to do that whole thing where you were going to pretend I had to go to the bathroom. I don't think I could have done it. I get super bladder shy, and I still don't even have to go. I think The Glorp is dehydrating me. I should probably drink some water.*

Uhhh okay. Yeah, can you see if the map is working while you do that? Mari reminded him.

The armored hyrax contingent moved off down the hall and out of sight. Greg moved up to the next bend to keep a lookout while Jerro and Mari consulted the map.

It was updating. The ink swirled and reformed, showing their current location, zoomed to scale and detailing out the chambers and passages. Mari noted the ones they had passed, building a reference to their current position. Across the top, the name changed from *The Glorp* to *The Citadel*.

"Can we see the other levels or zoom out on this?" Mari asked Jerro.

Jerro spread the map flat on the ground. "Maybe. Let me try something."

The two rodents, on all fours, carefully examined it.

"Okay, I think I've got it," Jerro said, focusing as his eyes rolled back. The map tilted from a bird's-eye plan to a side profile, then peeled through its levels as if responding to his intent. With the whites of his eyes still showing he continued. "Let's go toward the top, maybe?"

"Yeah," Mari said, locked on the white orbs. She shifted her attention back to the map. "If I were a big bad hyrax, I would definitely want to do my evil activities from the top."

"This is the spot." Mari pointed at a large chamber, one level spread wide at the top floor.

Greg's thought snapped. *Guys, someone is coming. Wrap it up and do that thing you were doing, Mari.*

Not sure I can do it again, Mari replied.

Jerro rolled up the map and slid it into his pack, and they hustled down the hall to catch up with Greg.

Mari reached into her mind again, searching for the illusion. She tried to find it the way she had learned, focusing on the carrot from her lesson and the certainty that it could exist even when it didn't.

Nothing came. Not even a flicker.

A small hyrax approached from down the hallway, slower than the others, posture folded in on itself. It kept glancing at the three friends as if it expected to be punished for simply standing there, then its eyes locked on Mari.

An instant later it startled and hopped backward into a corner, pressing itself into the stone, desperate to vanish.

A scream filled the hallway. It was still sharp and ugly, but there was a gentler quality beneath it, less threat than panic. The sound bounced off the tight stone, multiplied, and came back worse.

Mari lifted both paws and took a careful step forward. "It's okay," she breathed, even though she didn't know if the hyrax could understand her. She pressed a paw to her chest in a simple gesture, then lowered it again. She kept her movements slow. No sudden turns. No quick steps. No reaching.

The scream broke apart into a choked breath. The hyrax's eyes stayed wide, chest heaving as it darted its gaze between Mari, Jerro, and Greg, waiting for one of them to rush it.

Greg moved first, but not toward it. He eased back to the last corner they had passed, turning his body so he could watch the corridor behind them.

Jerro raised a paw to his temple, attention pulling inward. *Let me see if I can learn anything. Just a light peek. Enough to understand her motive, not enough to hurt her.*

Mari didn't answer. She kept approaching until she was close enough to share the corner without crowding it. Then she turned her back to the wall and slid down beside the hyrax, leaving a small gap between them. She sat still, paws resting in her lap, letting her breathing settle into something calm and steady.

The hyrax stayed pressed against the stone. Its fur looked duller than the others, rough in places, and its limbs trembled with exhausted fear. It quieted, but it didn't relax.

Jerro stepped closer, careful with his footfalls, and his expression shifted into that distant focus Mari had seen before. He was still in the hallway with them, but his mind moved somewhere else.

When Jerro entered the hyrax's mind, he hit the raw edge of panic first. Everything in her was scanning for danger and punishment. There was no language to follow, no words to translate, only sensation and expectation, fear worn into shape by repetition.

Corner. Trap. Big shapes. Consequence.

He held steady and eased past the surface, keeping his presence small and quiet. The jagged fear did not vanish, but it loosened enough for images to form.

He saw her in The Citadel's corridors, slipping aside before anyone had to ask. Always yielding space. Always a step behind. Shoved shoulders. A sharp sting, then the dull certainty that she wasn't wanted.

Work filled the gaps. The tasks no one claimed. Cleaning. Hauling. Scraping. Anything that kept her moving, head down, muscles burning—because being busy was safer than being noticed.

Loneliness sat under it all. Not new. Something older, deeper, never given the chance to heal.

Jerro pushed farther back, searching for where that grief began.

The Citadel fell away, and a different place rose into view. Rocky buff stone spread under an open sky. Tufts of green succulent vegetation clung to cracks in the stone, and wind moved cleanly through low scrub. The air there felt sharp and bright compared to the dead weight of The Glorp. In the memory, she was younger. Lighter. She wasn't alone. Her brother was there, close enough that her mind carried the steady comfort of him without having to look.

Then the birds came.

Enormous shadows swept across the rocks. Heavy wings, dust pluming at each landing, thick bills clacking like tools turned into weapons. A contingent of hyrax rode them, hard-eyed and sure of their authority. Jerro couldn't catch the meaning of what they said, but their intent was unmistakable.

Obedience.

On their armor, stamped and repeated, were the same three letters Jerro had seen earlier. I-R-S.

Her brother was forced forward. There was a moment where his body tensed, where he resisted, where his eyes flicked toward her with a silent promise that made her chest ache. Then numbers and threat crushed that moment into inevitability. They left anyway, pulled into service under the Overlord's banner, into allegiance she hated and could not stop.

Jerro pushed too far, and the memory flared. Pain and panic snapped back across the hyrax's thoughts, too sharp, too raw, threatening to drag her fear back into the hallway with them.

He pulled forward again, choosing a later thread.

The Citadel returned with rigid order. Training. Marching. Command. Her brother was there again, older now, shaped by constant pressure. He was preparing for a mission. She hovered near him, trying not to show her fear, trying to be the kind of sibling that made leaving easier instead of harder. The feeling she carried was clear enough to tighten Jerro's chest.

Don't go. Don't leave me here alone.

He left anyway. That was the way of The Citadel.

Jerro watched her wait through long hours and longer days. Birds returned. Riders returned. Her brother did not. The Overlord arrived when her brother did not, and The Citadel tightened around itself. Training intensified. Missions increased. Discipline sharpened into something crueler. She worked harder and kept her head down, doing odd jobs until her body ached, because grief didn't earn mercy here.

Then word reached her.

Jerro still couldn't understand what was said, not in any literal way, but he felt the message land in her like a blow. The shape of it. The finality delivered without softness.

Her brother had died.

The only reason offered was cold. He had died rescuing the Overlord.

Jerro's focus tightened painfully as realization hit. *Deepworks.* This was the same mission. The same event that had taken Keeper Aleese. The same wound that still burned inside him whenever he let his mind drift too close to it.

Anger surged, bright and immediate, tangled with something else that surprised him. *Recognition.* Not of her life, but of her position. Trapped in a machine that ground hyraxes into tools. Fed lies and cruel priorities until it all felt inevitable.

Jerro steadied himself. He didn't push deeper. He didn't need to. He brought his attention back toward the surface of her thoughts, toward the panic that had driven her into the corner, and he placed something small and careful there.

Not words. Not language. Just intent, clear and steady.

No harm. Not enemy. Pass through. Safe.

The hyrax's breathing shifted. It didn't become calm, not fully, but it stopped breaking apart. Her eyes flicked toward Jerro, then Mari, and the frantic edge softened just enough to leave room for choice.

Jerro opened his eyes and lowered his paw, expression tight with what he'd seen.

She's not like the others, Jerro sent. *She's terrified, and she's alone here. She lost her brother.* He held some of the details as his own, for now at least.

Mari didn't move. She stayed seated beside the hyrax, quiet and patient, letting the silence do the work her failed illusion could not.

Mari stood slowly. "Come on. Let's get moving."

As they continued, the passages became narrower, winding tighter and tighter as the floor area of each ascending level reduced with the structure of the spire.

Mari paused on a landing that opened through a narrow archway. Jerro and Greg stacked at the entryway behind her. Beyond it was a small round room, quieter than the halls, with a glowing projection suspended in the center above a low pedestal.

A web of connected pathways radiated outward from a single thick column, splitting into finer lines until terminating. Beneath it, a second network mirrored the first in reverse, reaching downward in pale branching strokes.

The image flickered as the lines rearranged themselves. Some segments brightened and softened, swelling with a hint of life, while others thinned to faint threads, then steadied again. Brief pulses of color moved through the web in different places at once, blooming and fading in slow cycles that didn't match each other.

A matte screen curved around the wall, and an array of controls lined a ledge below. The screen was marked with icons depicting locations. Contours indicated the terrain.

Jerro pulled out his map and zoomed out. Mari moved into the room, looking back at Jerro and Greg. "This is a navigation deck?"

Jerro followed and held the map up. "Definitely. Look at this."

They matched.

"Is that where The Citadel was heading then?" Greg pointed at a spot on the display, marked with a circle icon. A dashed trail traced the path of The Citadel, held centered.

"I'd assume so," Jerro said, consulting both maps beside Greg.

Mari turned back to the projection, lingering on it. The glow lit her face against the shadowed room. It felt familiar. Like a place she had been but couldn't remember.

Your return has been anticipated... A deeply disturbing voice penetrated their minds.

A shiver ran up their spines. They froze, eyes snapping to each other.

Nothing more followed.

Mari swallowed and started to speak. "Come on, let's..." She cleared her throat and steadied herself. "Let's get up there. We're almost there."

The ascent was marked by a stairway that spiraled along the exterior of the spire, enclosed by columns of metal and yellow sheets of energy, like those on the cell where they had left Phlip.

They rounded the final corner. A wide landing led to a fortress door. No seams or handle, just a dark slab waiting. Two armored guards wielded outstretched polearms, crossed in front of it. Without a word, they raised their weapons to a vertical position, and the door jarred, sliding upward into a pocket above.

The friends approached with trepidation, passed the guards, and entered the large chamber.

The ceiling was translucent, glass or energy shielding perhaps. It lit the room more than the rest of The Citadel. Beyond it, a dark blood-red sky pressed close. Three moons appeared in series, one yellow and two smaller ones with a green hue.

A cylindrical tube filled with translucent orange liquid bubbled. The Prince was suspended within the fluid column. His body was withered now, eyes closed.

Mari reached out telepathically, but there was nothing.

You won't have any luck with that one. I've separated his psionic essence from his corporeal being. The deep voice echoed, and unease swept through them in a wave.

Standing in the middle of the room toward the back was the large hyrax, the Overlord. Outstretched and upturned paws revealed a cube floating above his right paw, glowing hot white, brimming with energy.

Without consent, the Overlord's voice tore into their minds again. The violation came first, then the aftertaste of it, a sour metallic dread that made their own thoughts slip loose. *Powerful that one was. This bounty will serve its purpose.*

The door dropped shut, slamming into the floor with such force it knocked Jerro off balance. He dropped to a knee.

As the Overlord turned with a flourish of his cape, an altar was briefly revealed, and the hairless creature lay flat upon it.

Jerro recovered and pulled his monocular down in front of his eye to confirm his suspicion. The hairless creature was the source of the unique signature he had seen earlier when tracking through The Glorp.

The Overlord's voice boomed through their minds, heavy enough to drive them down.

Now, my fragmented kin, we find out how much you have remembered!

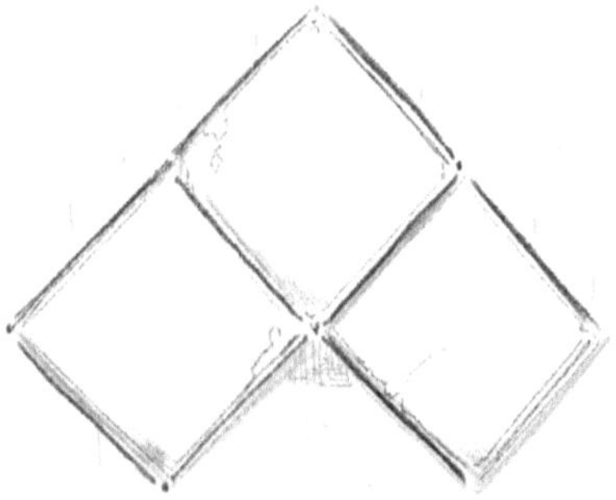

CHAPTER 16 | ANNIHILATION

The massive chamber trembled. Crimson light bled through the translucent ceiling above, but it felt distant, thinned as if it had passed through layers before it could reach them. Darkness pooled in the room anyway, deep and unnatural, pressing in where it shouldn't have. As the three friends pushed themselves upright, a metallic, dusty tang hit Mari's nose, industrial and oily. By instinct, they forced their psionosense back into place. The room resolved in fits and starts, not cleanly, but enough to reveal the lattice of forces holding it together and the dense distortions embedded within.

A clever trick, the Overlord's voice rippled through their minds.

He was nowhere to be seen. Not above, not behind, not even within the web of psionic architecture they strained to perceive. His presence felt smeared across the room itself, woven into the walls and air. Then, without warning, his signature reappeared, overlapping their own and pressing inward from every direction at once.

Greg swore, and they snapped together on instinct, backs touching, paws drawn close. The space around them tightened. Their bodies compressed inward, joints locking, breath driven from their chests as an invisible force twisted them together. Pain flared, sharp and disorienting, collapsing thought into noise.

The Overlord stepped into view directly in front of them, his massive frame solidifying from the distortion. He stood on a raised platform marked by three overlapping triangles and a nine-point star. Jerro's stomach tightened at the sight, recognition sparking before he could place why.

"I thought things would be more interesting this time," he said, his voice carrying both sound and pressure. "It seems that you have remembered nothing."

The force increased. Mari felt her ribs strain, her spine bowing under the pressure. Her vision blurred, then steadied as her gaze drifted upward despite herself, drawn toward the ceiling. Beyond the fractured slate clouds, the three moons hung low and swollen in the sky. The clouds moved, folding and reshaping with deliberate slowness.

At first, she thought it was another trick. Then she saw the outline take form. The broad muzzle. The incisors. The long fur trailing like mist.

The old marmot's face emerged from the clouds, calm and impossibly familiar.

The Burrowing Rodent Empire exists within, the voice pressed through the chaos, quieter than the Overlord but far heavier. *This vessel carries on. An eternal dig. A burrow with no end.*

The words were not new. They were not instructions. They were structure. *Intent.*

Mari stopped fighting the pressure.

Instead of pushing outward, she let the phrase settle, letting it define her shape the way Jerro had taught her stone should be read, not forced. She felt the Overlord's hold slip, not break, but lose coherence, like a grip tightened around something that no longer resisted.

The pain vanished.

She could move.

So could Jerro. So could Greg.

Their awareness snapped inward, then outward, collapsing into a single shared frame. No words passed between them. They did not need to. The same voice had touched all three, threading them together—a singular, aligned consciousness.

Mari lifted first, rising gently as Greg and Jerro rotated around her, their positions locking into symmetry without discussion. The shape formed naturally, something Mari recognized from the mosaic and the nested diamond symbol she had seen before. Three diamond anchors circumscribed within a sphere of focused force.

Annihilation.

The Overlord's expression shifted. Confidence drained from his face, replaced by something sharp and animalistic.

He turned and gestured toward the massive stone door, space folding around him as it opened. The two guards outside leaned in, startled.

Mari reached out, not with force, but with certainty.

The door slammed shut inches from the Overlord's grasp.

He turned back toward them slowly, eyes wide now as he took in the formation hovering at the center of the chamber.

"Well," he said, voice tightening. "Perhaps I was wrong this time."

He vanished in a flash of distortion and reappeared beside the altar, already reaching for the cube of energy he had drained from the Prince. He pulled it into his grasp and crushed it inward. The cube dissolved into swirling particulate, drawn into his body in a violent surge.

Cracks crawled across his skin as the energy fought for space within him. Blue and red light burst through the fractures, swirling and overtaking his form until the red glow consumed him entirely.

He laughed, the sound tearing through the chamber and reverberating through The Citadel itself.

The Overlord drew power from everywhere at once. From the chamber. From the plane. From the structure beneath their feet. The blast that followed was blinding, so intense it stripped even their shared perception into static.

When the dust settled, half of the chamber was gone.

The sphere was gone.

"Typical," the Overlord muttered, surveying the destruction with satisfaction.

Above him, the ceiling screamed.

A streak of white-hot energy tore downward, carrying the friends within it. They pierced through the Overlord and the floor beneath him in the same instant, driving straight down through The Citadel's core. Floor after floor shattered as they cut through the structure without slowing, Jerro holding the geometry steady, Greg timing the descent, Mari anchoring the alignment.

For a single suspended moment, they saw the Overlord's face again, terror fully unmasked.

Then they were gone.

The impact at The Citadel's base sent a ripple through The Glorp. A singularity formed where the structure met the ground, metal and stone folding inward as the fortress consumed itself.

The sphere burst upward into the blood-red sky.

Phlip.

The thought formed once, shared and immediate. They did not need to search. They knew exactly where he was.

They struck the containment hall in a controlled crash, the spire tilting violently around them as yellow energy fields flickered and failed. Cells opened one by one.

The formation dissolved, and they hovered apart, separate once more, though the power did not entirely leave them. Blue light flared across their foreheads, forming the crest of three diamonds bound by a circle.

Mari hit the ground running.

Phlip's field collapsed just as she reached him. He hopped forward and crashed into her chest, licking her face with frantic relief.

"Phlip," she breathed, burying her face in his fur.

Greg glanced toward the corner cell, searching for the mushroom, but it was gone.

"We need to move," he said. "The Prince and the furless one."

Mari nodded, already turning. "Can you get them?"

Jerro grinned, breathless. "Yeah. I think so."

Greg pointed toward the horizon, where a small white dome stood alone against cracked earth. Mari's breath caught.

My dream.

"Meet me there," she said. "Hurry."

They shot skyward, streaks of blue-white energy cutting through the red sky.

A small voice trembled behind her.

"Awawa?"

The young hyrax stood in the doorway, eyes wide and uncertain.

Mari hesitated only a moment, then waved her over. The hyrax ran to her without hesitation.

She swung up onto Phlip's back and pulled the hyrax in behind her. "Hold on," she murmured.

Phlip leapt from the collapsing spire, and Mari poured her power into him. His legs found air. They were flying.

Behind them, The Citadel folded into itself. Birds scattered. Riders fled. None pursued.

They landed at the temple as the dust wave surged closer. The floor split, and the all-season tree rose gently into place, roots gripping the floating land.

Greg and Jerro arrived moments later, burdened but victorious, carrying the Prince and the bare creature, both unconscious and alive.

Mari ushered them aboard just as The Glorp gave way entirely.

The island drifted free into the quiet darkness of space.

Stars filled the void.

Exhaustion claimed them one by one as they lay together beneath the branches of the all-season tree, floating silently onward.

CHAPTER 17 | PARITY

A warm light stirred Mari from sleep. She lay tangled among a mismatched pile of bodies on the small island, its soil bound together by the gnarled roots of the all-season tree. For a moment she stayed still, listening to the quiet rhythm of breathing around her, letting the warmth settle into her bones.

When she finally rose and stretched, the motion felt unhurried and easy, as if her body had decided on its own that rest had been sufficient. It took only a few steps to reach the edge of the island. Mari peered down and felt a faint disorientation as the jungle spread beneath her, familiar and distant all at once.

Behind her, she could hear Jerro and Greg beginning to stir.

Their ship lingered below, just where they had left it, resting in the clearing like a patient animal waiting to be tended. Scars from the battle still marked the surrounding ground, broken chitin and scorched foliage littered the jungle.

Had this really been only a lune ago? Mari wondered.

"Mari…"

The voice came weakly from behind her.

She turned at once. Prince Lukyaza sat slumped at the base of the tree, his once-commanding form reduced to something fragile and strained. Relief flared through her, quickly followed by concern as she crossed the island toward him, slowing as she drew near, unsure where to touch or whether touching would do more harm than good.

"Lukyaza," she said softly.

Jerro was already moving, dropping to one knee beside the Prince. Greg followed, quieter than usual, his attention fixed on Lukyaza's labored breathing.

"I… I'm uncertain how you accomplished it," Lukyaza said, his voice catching as he spoke. "But you have my eternal gratitude for resc—"

His words broke apart in a fit of coughing that left his body trembling.

"Water," Jerro said urgently. Greg was already reaching into Jerro's pack, pulling free the pitcher and passing it over. Jerro supported Lukyaza's head as he took a careful sip, the effort clearly costing him more than it should have.

The Prince lifted one trembling paw and reached toward Mari's forehead. His claws brushed the faintly glowing emblem there.

"That mark…" he murmured. "I have seen this befo—"

Another coughing spasm cut him off, harsher than the last.

"It's alright," Mari said gently, placing a paw on his shoulder. *We can use our minds. Just send your message. You don't need to strain yourself.*

There was no response. Only the sound of his breathing, shallow and uneven.

When Lukyaza opened his eyes again, they drifted past Mari and settled on the furless figure lying nearby.

"The human," he said faintly, his head tilted and eyes locked on the tall, smooth-skinned figure. "You saved it as well?"

"Human?" Greg echoed, glancing between the others.

Mari nodded. "I guess so. We couldn't just leave them there."

At that, Lukyaza's gaze shifted to the small hyrax standing close to the human's side. The creases in his brow wrinkled. He looked back at Mari. "You cannot bring them ba—"

The sentence collapsed into a wheezing gasp. His breathing grew more labored, each inhale drawn out and thin. The friends spoke softly, reassuring him, though none of them knew whether their words reached him anymore.

Lukyaza's eyes closed, then opened once more. He looked at Mari, then at Jerro and Greg, and a small, tired smile crossed his face. A long breath left his chest.

Stillness followed.

Do not trust them.

The words drifted through the mindspace, faint but unmistakable, and then faded.

Mari's vision blurred. Jerro placed a paw against Lukyaza's chest. Greg rested his paw over Jerro's, and after a moment Mari added hers to the small stack. They closed their eyes together, offering a silent farewell. This was the way of The Burrow. A quiet acknowledgment of a life that had reached its end.

Mari looked up at her friends. "We burrow."

Greg and Jerro repeated it with her.

Lukyaza's body crumbled, breaking apart into a fine, pale dust that lifted gently into the air. The breeze carried it around the branches of the all-season tree before dispersing it into the warm morning haze.

Across the island, the human stirred.

The small hyrax beside them startled, hopping sideways with a soft, alarmed sound. She turned her pointed snout toward the human, eyes wide, one small fang catching the light as she watched for signs of danger.

In unison, the three friends turned.

Up close, the human was stranger than Mari had expected. Not a trace of fur covered its body. Their skin looked soft and vulnerable, wrapped in a single rough garment that covered their torso and upper legs. It seemed hastily made, likely fashioned by hyrax paws.

"I feel like we're supposed to do something," Greg whispered. "I just don't know what that is."

The human extended an arm, long fingers unfolding toward the hyrax. After a moment's hesitation, she stepped closer and pressed herself into the offered hand, nuzzling against it with a familiarity that surprised Mari.

Jerro exhaled slowly. "So are we trusting them, or was Lukyaza warning us about something else entirely?"

I don't know, Mari replied without speaking, watching the pair closely. *This human. This is an Ancient. What I saw in the cave back in Long Valley.* She made a small, open-palmed gesture toward them and let her posture soften.

Careful Mari, Jerro sent along with an analytic glance.

Mari crouched beside the hyrax. Its long, sausage-like body squirmed with nervous energy, movements sharp and uncontained. Mari lowered herself slowly and rested a paw against its side, careful not to startle it. The tension didn't vanish, but it softened, the frantic motion resolving into smaller, uncertain shifts.

"Squiggy?" she murmured, not as a question meant to be answered, but as something that felt right to offer.

The hyrax tilted its head, then hopped forward, pressing into Mari's fur and holding there. Mari smiled and let her paw settle more firmly against its back.

"Seems fitting." Greg glanced back at the human. "And what about this one, the human… The Ancient?"

Jerro hesitated. "They remind me of something. Old rat lore. The Cult of the Bound One. They believed shedding fur brought them closer to power."

Mari waved that off. "That's just a story."

"After everything we've seen," Jerro said, already moving closer to the human, "I'm not ruling anything out."

He placed a paw against his chest. "Jerro." Then pointed to Mari. "Mari." Then to Greg. "Greg."

The human watched him closely.

"Jerro," the human said slowly, placing their bare hand on his head. The word came out rough, but unmistakable.

Jerro smiled broadly and turned back to the others. "It can learn."

He hesitated, then added, "I'm going to try something."

Jerro touched a paw to his temple and reached.

The moment his awareness crossed the threshold, he felt it.

Nothing.

No structure. No surface thoughts. Just an open, dark expanse that stretched outward without edges. It made his chest tighten, but curiosity pulled him deeper. In the emptiness, something shifted. Patterns formed, subtle at first, then more defined. Curving ridges. Harmonic waveforms that reminded him of the anomalous frequency he had detected in the Glorp.

They were beautiful. Hypnotic.

Jerro felt himself drifting, spiraling inward, the sensation of falling slow and endless.

"Jerro!"

Paws grabbed him, shaking him hard enough to snap the world back into focus. He lay on the cool earth, gasping.

"The pattern," he murmured. "Where did it go?"

He scrambled to his feet and stared at the human, flipping down his monocular in a reflexive motion. The device felt inadequate now, like a child's toy.

He tried to reach again—to recreate the sensation.

Nothing answered.

Mari stepped in front of him, her voice steady. "We need rest. Whatever that was, it's not something we're meant to solve right now."

Greg nodded. "We're alive. That's enough for today."

Jerro let out a slow breath and stepped back. The human watched him with open, unguarded eyes, no sign of intent or understanding, only quiet curiosity.

The island had continued to descend while they spoke. By now it hovered only a few tails above the jungle floor, settling near the clearing where their ship waited.

"Phlip?" Mari called suddenly.

A moment later, Phlip bounded into view from the spring side of the island, his face stained green from fresh foliage, a bundle of grass still clutched in his mouth. Mari sighed, shaking her head as he trotted past.

Together, they disembarked.

The jungle was quiet as they crossed the clearing. Too quiet, Mari thought, though she couldn't say why. The insect creatures they had fought earlier were gone, leaving only broken foliage and scorched ground behind. It felt as if the land itself was holding its breath.

Jerro moved ahead instinctively, already slipping back into familiar roles. He assessed the ship's damage with a quick circuit, muttering to himself as he went, then began assigning tasks with practiced ease. Mari took the cockpit with Phlip close at her side. Greg headed for the weapons systems. Jerro waved Squiggy and the human over, attempting to include them, giving them a simple collection task.

In the end, their contribution amounted to a loosely organized pile of scrap that included hull fragments, firewood, smooth jungle stones, and several half-eaten pieces of fruit. Squiggy seemed pleased with the result. The human simply watched, occasionally handing her something she had already set down.

Mari worked through the cockpit damage carefully, rewiring severed controls while Phlip assisted in his own way by offering her the wrong tools at exactly the wrong times. She thanked him anyway. Greg crawled through the weapons bay, checking the turret tracks and coaxing partial life back into the shielding.

Jerro disappeared into the engine room.

When the hamster reactor hummed back to life, the sound brought an unexpected tightness to his chest. Lunda's presence returned with it, her attunement snapping into place, seamless and immediate.

Jerro, it is a relief to be with you again. Lunda's calming voice moved through his mind.

He told her everything as they worked. About The Glorp. About The Citadel. About Prince Lukyaza. About the power they had touched and barely understood. Lunda listened with rapt focus, asking questions that revealed just how much she had missed while the connection had been severed. She knew nothing of The Glorp and noted that she would record his account in her database. That absence alone felt unsettling.

Despite their progress, the propulsion system refused to respond. The control unit had taken the worst of the quantum pulsar surge during the initial skirmish. Jerro traced the failure twice before conceding what he already knew.

They were not leaving under their own power.

A shadow crossed the clearing without warning, darkening the entirety of the space.

Mari noticed it first from the cockpit. She looked up just in time to see the sun eclipsed by the smooth silver curve of an enormous parabolic ship hovering low in the atmosphere. A sphere of crackling energy pulsed within the open interior of its frame, contained and deliberate.

Guys, she sent. *You need to see this.*

Jerro and Greg emerged onto the deck as Mari and Phlip joined them.

"What is that?" Jerro asked quietly.

"I don't know," Mari replied.

A second vessel approached. Smaller, but sharing the same parabolic design, rotated ninety degrees to descend vertically. A pale white energy trace followed its controlled descent.

Jerro shifted his stance. "We don't have much left if this turns unfriendly."

Greg nodded. "Barely enough to make it loud."

The smaller ship settled near the site where Lukyaza had last stood. Three figures emerged from a portal beneath it, descending slowly as their cloaks rippled in the humid air. The same crest Lukyaza and his guardians had worn marked the hull. A braided circle framing a hollow triangle.

Jerro's ears lifted. "Borruki."

Greg leaned against the railing. "Hopefully, the helpful kind."

The central figure moved ahead of the others, taller, more assured. When it drew close, it lowered its hood, revealing features similar to Lukyaza's, though aged and refined. The two flanking figures remained armored beneath their cloaks, silent and watchful.

The Borruki leader spoke in the same warbled language Lukyaza had used. Mari shook her head. The figure reached into its cloak, withdrawing a translation unit and activated it with a practiced turn.

"Greetings," it said smoothly. "I am Inquisitor Tuyaza."

His gaze flicked briefly to Squiggy. Then to the human.

Mari felt something tighten in her chest.

"What are you doing here Inquisitor?" She asked sharper than she had intended.

Jerro and Greg glanced at her, surprised by the shift in tone.

"We are a recovery team," Tuyaza replied evenly. "Searching for members of our order who failed to report in. Three, to be precise. Have you encountered any others of our kind recently?"

"No," Mari said at once.

Jerro and Greg both looked at her.

Lukyaza warned us, she sent. *I don't know who he meant, but until we do, we only trust each other.*

Tuyaza inclined his head slightly. "Then I must ask, who are you, and why are you in our system?"

Jerro stepped forward. "We crashed here. Reactor is intact. Propulsion is not."

Tuyaza examined the damage with a practiced eye. "That aligns with what I see. I will mark your vessel as non-hostile to prevent further incident."

He dismissed the display with a casual motion and turned back toward his ship.

Mari called out. "Wait… Can you help us repair it?"

Tuyaza paused. Slowly, he turned back. "Certainly. We will transport you to our forward base where repairs can be completed."

I thought we weren't trusting them. Jerro transmitted hesitantly.

Mari exhaled quietly. *We don't have any other options.*

The larger ship maneuvered into position, tractor fields engaging. Their vessel lifted from the jungle floor as twilight crept across the sky faster than it should have.

Hours later, Greg stirred the others. "I think we're there." Although completely spent, he had been unable to calm his mind and rest with the others. He held a long blue stick — one of the vectorization rakes Ferdi had issued them on Station. It seemed he had figured out how to use it. The fur along his spine was combed into neat grooves.

Any trace of daylight had faded fully, and starlight dominated now. The moon wasn't out yet, and a deep, quiet darkness permeated the jungle below, the kind that made shapes feel imagined until they moved. Above them, the sky was clean and sharp, scattered with stars that looked too bright for how little comfort they offered. Their ship drifted beneath the looming parabolic hull, suspended in its wake like a small thing being carried somewhere it hadn't agreed to go. The air seemed thicker at night, heavy with humidity and sound, every distant call and snap arriving late and wrong. Even the glow from the Borruki craft felt cold, a controlled light that did not soften anything, only revealed how much more there was to hide.

Ahead, elongated slivers of light formed a vast ring around a tower that stretched upward into orbit. Energy flowed rhythmically between the structures, cycling with methodical precision.

The towing vessel veered away as the tower took control, drawing their ship toward its foundation. A translucent blue tube extended to meet their deck. The smaller crescent ship docked nearby, its own tube connecting in parallel.

Inquisitor Tuyaza and his guardians were already descending.

Squiggy moved closer to the human, pressing herself against their side. Mari noticed the way the human instinctively angled their body to shelter her, a quiet, unspoken agreement between them.

Whatever evil had shaped the hyrax, Mari thought to herself, *it had not claimed this one yet.*

They stepped into the tube as one. The light folded around them as the tower drew closer.

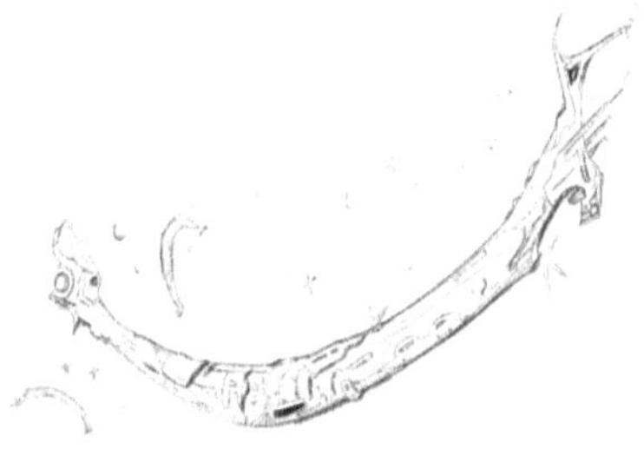

CHAPTER 18 | HOMEWARD

The group moved down the ramp, strung out in a line. Mari led the way, followed closely by Phlip, then Jerro, then Greg, who walked beside him. Behind them, by several tails, trailed the human and Squiggy. She had perched on the human's shoulder, and the furless creature carried her with steady patience that made the arrangement feel strangely natural—like they had done it before.

As they moved, energy bursts rippled down the tube walkway toward their ship and returned toward the towers in waves. It reminded Mari of their approach to the complex, that same pulse and reply, like the whole place was breathing through conduits instead of lungs.

At the end of the walkway, they reached a nexus with openings to a dozen other tubes. Most were retracted and sealed, dark mouths closed tight, but the one next to theirs dilated and produced the Inquisitor and two guardians. Above them, the center of the ceiling expanded, spreading outward. A platform descended and stopped flush with their floor. Another six guardians stood motionless along the perimeter, garbed in the same powered armor and bearing the Borruki crest on their left breastplate, but lacking cloaks.

"The Queen Regent would like to meet you all," the Inquisitor said plainly, gesturing toward the platform as if he were inviting them to dinner.

Mari glanced back at her friends, then at the Inquisitor. "Uhhh, I'm not sure about that. What if we just get our ship repaired and be on our way? We really don't want to be a bother or anything."

"I insist. It is no bother," the Inquisitor replied, reinforcing the gesture by raising his brow line with a practiced calm that made Mari's stomach tighten.

The friends looked at each other, sharing unease through the mindspace. They all felt the same conclusion settle, heavy and unpleasant. They did not have a choice. This wasn't a request.

Together, they stepped onto the platform. The guardians shifted with them, surrounding the group in a loose ring that could tighten in a second. The Inquisitor and his two guardians joined as well.

The ceiling opened again. The platform accelerated rapidly upward into the tower's interior. Floor after floor flashed by too quickly to make out details. Mari tried anyway, watching for patterns, exits, anything she could anchor to, but the tower swallowed the view as soon as it offered it.

When the platform stopped, it did so abruptly yet smooth, the kind of motion that reminded Mari of a well-tuned machine. They stood in a large circular room. The outer walls were lined with windows that gave a full view of the planet below. They were high enough that the curvature was unmistakable—the landscape bending away into haze.

Several large columns encircled the interior. Ornate banners hung around them. Toward the bottom, where the fabric tapered to a point, the emblem of the Borruki rested. Heroic imagery shifted to life across the body of the cloth. Borruki struck confident poses against backgrounds that alternated between ceremony and war, between clean light and ruined ground.

Directly ahead, a wide set of steps led up to a sleek metal throne. The architecture was cohesive in a way that felt almost oppressive, as if every angle and surface had been designed to remind visitors that this place did not tolerate improvisation. Even the guardians' armor matched the room, from the plating to the seams.

Atop the throne sat a tall Borruki with softer features than Lukyaza or the others they had met. A diadem rested on her head, the central gem swirling with shifting hues that moved from cool shades into warmer ones and back again. A fitted emerald robe draped her body and overflowed onto the throne like pooled fabric.

Mari held the stare. Held the moment. The regal figure's irises were a soft violet that seemed to glow at the edges—not bright, but present, like a warning you only noticed after it had already affected you.

Two guardians in ornately engraved armor and flowing cloaks flanked the throne at floor level, rigid and silent.

The Inquisitor moved through the group with a grace that felt rehearsed and approached the throne. He took a knee and addressed her with deep respect, speaking in the Borruki language.

The Queen placed a translation disc on her temple and dialed it. "Please, let us speak so that our guests may understand as well. Did you encounter any faction resistance?"

The Inquisitor turned his torso slightly, still holding eye contact with her. He gestured toward the group, presenting them as evidence. "As you wish, my Queen. Surface tension has escalated. We intercepted two Grishki skiffs patrolling the equatorial region. Regrettably, I have been unsuccessful in locating Prince Lukyaza. However, I do return with a recent development."

"Approach and tell me more," the Queen said, breaking her gaze with the Inquisitor and looking back toward the group.

"Come forward and present yourselves," Tuyaza ordered.

They did so. Guardians flanked their movement, not touching, but close enough that Mari could feel the space being managed around them.

"Kneel before the Queen," the Inquisitor commanded.

"That is unnecessary," the Queen said immediately, dismissing his command with a subtle wave of her paw. Tuyaza's expression flickered. It was small, but Mari caught it. Surprise, then control.

The Queen studied them as they stood there, surrounded by armor and glass and the curvature of a world beneath their feet.

"When you met my son, what did he tell you?" she asked bluntly.

Mari felt Jerro and Greg hold still beside her. Their faces went neutral in the same way. Their bodies did not. Mari's heart was pounding in her chest.

How did she know? Mari sent. *Is she in here with us?*

The Queen's lips formed a sharp grin. *My dear children. If you resist, this will be rather unpleasant for yourselves and your friends.*

Her voice did not travel through the air. It entered their minds with cold precision and stabbing pain.

The pain rippled through Mari's thoughts, echoing through her body like a second heartbeat made of needles. She looked over her shoulder and saw the same expression on Greg and Jerro. They were feeling it too, the shared reality of it. Squiggy pressed herself tighter against the human's shoulder, her limbs trembling, and the human lifted a hand slowly, not in defense, but in instinct, resting its furless palm against Squiggy's back as if the touch itself could ground her.

"Enough of this!" Mari shouted, rage rising in her throat. Blue-white fire flared behind her eyes, and the circumscribed diamond emblem on her forehead matched their intensity.

"NO."

The Queen's voice boomed through the chamber. The air compressed and distorted. A force wave rippled outward, throwing the group back as time dilated and slowed, then snapped back into place as if reality had been yanked tight.

Mari was first up, with Greg and Jerro right behind her. She tried to channel a mind blast directly at the Queen.

Nothing came.

The Queen held up a small metallic sphere. A red ring glowed around its circumference, and it produced a low hum that was barely audible, but the effect was immediate. The sound did not stop their thoughts. It drowned them. Mari felt her mind pushing against it like lungs fighting water, every attempt to reach the mindspace turning into a suffocating strain.

"I thought you might try something like that," the Queen said calmly. "Now, if you will, I have questions to which I would like answers."

The guardians had returned to their feet. Several drew short blades and tightened their perimeter. If it was not clear before, it was now. This was not a meeting. It was containment.

"Shackle their minds," the Queen directed, her tone precise.

Tuyaza gestured with an open paw. Four guardians produced metallic collars and opened them with a quick flick of the wrist.

Greg shoved the guardian who approached him. Two more stepped in immediately, grappling Greg's arms and slamming him onto the cold metal floor. A third pressed the collar around his neck. It scaled automatically, and the red ring activated with a pulse that made Greg's body jerk once.

Mari, Jerro, and Squiggy did not resist. Mari watched Squiggy's eyes dart, terrified, but the little hyrax held still, pressed close to the human until a guardian guided her away and placed the collar around her neck with the same detached efficiency used for fitting a part to equipment.

Noticeably, they did not collar the human. They did not even attempt it. The guardians treated the furless creature as a secured item already accounted for.

Mari tried again to reach into the mindspace.

A wall had been built there. Impenetrable and infinite.

The Queen deactivated the sphere and placed it on a small table adjacent to the throne. "Now," she said, returning to her previous tone with sharper emphasis, "what did my son tell you when you met him in the jungle?"

Mari stared into the Queen's eyes. She blinked quickly, looked away, then forced herself back into that violet gaze.

"He told us he was looking for a relic," Mari said, the words catching before they came free. "An artifact."

"Good," the Queen replied. "That was not so hard, was it?" She tilted her head. "Did he mention its purpose?"

"No," Mari responded quickly. "He just said it was created and hidden by the original Borruki millions of years ago when they settled here."

The frustration she had been holding broke through anyway, spilling out sharp and hot. "What is it even? He didn't find anything. We ran into these hyrax—they were the reason for his death. We were trying to help. We brought him back from that place. The Glorp."

The Queen's gaze narrowed into a squint that felt more like focus than emotion.

"So," she said after a long pause, "Lukyaza is dead then."

"Well, that does change things," she added, her eyes shifting toward Tuyaza.

Mari noticed what the Queen did not ask. Nothing about The Glorp. Nothing about the hyrax. Mari felt it press against her ribs like a hard object. *Did she already know?* She thought. *Or did she not care?*

"Mari," the Queen said, returning her attention with a clinical steadiness, "you and your friends were an unexpected variable. It seems you have proven useful despite your ignorance. Under different circumstances, you may have even proven yourselves worthy allies in the coming conflicts." She paused only long enough for the words to land. "Inquisitor, take the human up for extraction. Dematerialize the rest of them."

"What?" Mari's voice broke on the word. "You said we helped wh–"

The Queen lifted an empty paw and closed it into a tight fist.

Mari's chest heaved, seized from the inside. Her voice was dragged back down into her throat. She could not speak. She could only choke on the shape of her own protest.

"Do not worry," Tuyaza whispered with a quiet smile as he shoved Mari back toward the platform. "You will be with the heretic prince again shortly."

From behind the throne, a cloaked figure hobbled out.

A wooden cane, twisted and warped, clacked against the metallic floor. The rhythm was uneven—the sound of old damage carried into present motion. A large flat tail protruded from the cloak.

Jerro's body went rigid.

A guardian struck him from behind, the blow snapping his head forward. Jerro stumbled, vision flaring white, then dark.

The cloaked figure leaned toward the Queen, whispering. Mari couldn't hear the words over the pulse in her own ears.

Jerro forced his eyes open. Through the blur, he looked up at the throne.

The figure turned its head toward them.

Worn silver fur. A scar that split across a patched eye. The shape of the face, the posture, the weight of authority held without effort.

Jerro's mouth opened, but no sound came. His throat tightened as recognition hit with a force that had nothing to do with the guardian's strike.

Ordinate Rull? This thought was drowned out by the collar. It would only be known to Jerro.

Another strike from behind sent his vision back into darkness.

Mari watched as two guardians flanked the human and guided it onto the platform. The human did not struggle. It simply turned its head once, slowly, looking back toward Squiggy. She strained against the guardians separating her, making a small, broken sound that did not become a word. The human lifted its hand as far as the guardians allowed and held it there, palm open, as if promising it would return even if it did not understand what promise it was making.

The platform shot upward into the core of the tower. The human vanished as the portal rotated and sealed the path with a smooth, indifferent motion.

Greg's gaze locked onto Mari. His dark brown eyes glazed and welled, but the grief did not get to finish forming. His expression shifted as his focus moved past Mari, past her shoulder, looking through her.

Mari assumed he was looking at Jerro and turned her head to check on him.

She realized it was not Jerro Greg was watching.

Their ship was slowly emerging into view beyond the long strip of windows across the chamber, rising from below like a predator surfacing from deep water. It moved with deliberate control. Both fore-and-aft turrets rotated toward the windows and held there, aligning with cold precision.

Jerro's vision returned in painful flashes. Warm blood ran through his fur and into his focus. From his prone position, he followed Mari and Greg's gaze and saw the ship's silhouette settle into place outside the glass.

Greg's voice tore through the room. "GET DOWN!"

He tackled Squiggy to the floor just as the first barrage hit.

Energy blasts ripped through the strip of windows, lighting the entire chamber as psionic pulses crackled into columns and stone. Glass shattered outward and inward. Shrapnel rained through the air, chunks of metal and stone spinning and screaming as they fell. Guardians were struck and sent reeling across the floor. Banners tore free and caught fire, revealing the columns they had veiled.

The barrage was relentless. Pulses ricocheted off the floor and ceiling, turning the throne room into a storm of light and debris with no safe center.

Mari grabbed Phlip and hauled him behind the far side of a nearby column. Jerro staggered after them, using it as cover while the guardians tried to return fire. Their powered suits drove them forward in heavy, deliberate strides, but turret fire broke their shields and cut them down before they could close the distance.

Across the room, Greg and Squiggy found refuge behind another column. Squiggy pressed herself into the stone, trembling, and Greg kept his body angled between her and the open space as if his own frame could be a shield.

The Queen still sat on her throne with the cloaked figure at her side. A force field shimmered around them, absorbing the assault with an eerie steadiness. The light from the impacts played across the Queen's emerald robe without changing her posture. She did not flinch.

Tuyaza and the last remaining guardian pressed themselves against a narrow section of windowless wall near the lift, using a concavity in the architecture to create shadowed cover from the ship's onslaught. Turret fire focused on the Queen and Tuyaza's positions, suppressing their action.

"Let's go!" Mari shouted toward Greg, pushing her voice above the roar.

Greg patted Squiggy quickly, and they sprinted.

Mari, Jerro, and Phlip were already moving. They ran at full speed across the open floor toward the windows. Their ship hovered outside, positioned within two tails of the broken frame. It was a long jump, especially now, and the collars made their psionics feel like they were wrapped in wire.

Mari reached the edge first and stopped just long enough to make sure Jerro and Phlip went ahead. Jerro leapt and caught the ship's deck with a hard landing. Phlip followed with ease, clearing Jerro's landing spot and helping him to his feet.

Greg and Squiggy followed. Greg was faster than any of them, but he stayed behind Squiggy, shepherding her through the chaos so she did not get swallowed by it.

They were close. A few more tails and they would be on the deck, and then the sky, and then away.

A strong paw grabbed Greg's ankle and yanked.

Greg slammed onto the floor with a thud. Pain flared through his ribs and up his spine, sharp enough to turn his stomach. He tried to inhale and it came in broken pieces. One of the guardians that had been struck down lay on its side, half-conscious, eyes locked on Greg with stubborn survival.

The guardian pulled Greg back, but Greg reacted instantly. He wrapped his legs around the guardian's neck and locked in, squeezing like a constrictor. The struggle lasted only moments before the guardian's grip loosened and its head fell back.

Greg panted, breath harsh in his chest, and then Mari's voice cut through the noise, raw with panic. "Greg. Greg! GREG!"

Greg's focus snapped back to her. He released the guardian, spun to his feet, and sprinted. He took the leap in stride, landing hard on the deck with a slide.

Jerro and Greg reached down and hauled Mari aboard.

Mari did not pause long enough to feel relief. She pointed toward the cockpit. "Go check the turrets and see what's up. I'm taking Phlip and Squiggy forward to see who's flying this thing."

They split without argument.

The ship pulled away from the building and gained altitude quickly, punching into thicker air as it climbed. The glow of the tower fell away beneath them.

Mari burst into the cockpit and found a singular hamster behind the controls, barely able to see out the window. It turned to Mari with a grin and shouted over the rattle of the ship, "Welcome back aboard, captain! She's all yours. But you gotta come take it, because if I let go I'm pretty sure I'll fall."

Its small body dangled by a single paw from the controls as the ship's angle of attack shifted and gravity pressed sideways through the cockpit. A smaller version of the control circlet rested around the hamster's head.

"You guys are heroes," Mari said, forcing her way across the angled floor.

Relieving the Derf, she took the controls and leveled the ship enough to stabilize.

The hamster scrambled up onto her shoulder and produced a small multi-tool. "Let me help you. I think I can get that collar off."

It worked quickly. Metal clicked. The collar released and fell to the floor.

"Alrighty, that should do it," the Derf said. "I've gotta get back to the engine room if we want any chance of making it out of here." It scurried off, disappearing through the hatch.

Lunda's reassuring presence rushed into their minds, filling the space where fear had been accumulating. *I'm so glad you all made it back safely. I felt our connection sever and knew we needed to do something. So I got the Derfs to help me execute a rescue. First, we repaired the ship. That proved easy after I hacked into the Borruki network and channeled their energy supply. The hamsters fabricated the parts from there. It was all quite simple, actually.*

You're amazing, Lunda, Jerro sent, his thought riding on equal parts relief and disbelief. *These hamsters are mad lads. I couldn't get the Derf off the turret.*

Greg joined in from the fore turret. *Yeah, this one just kept blasting until I ripped it off the seat by force.*

Mari exhaled shakily and turned her attention inward, reaching for the chronoarch the way Rufus had taught her. *Alright. Let's get out of here.*

It came quicker than last time. Natural, reflexive, almost like the motion had been waiting behind her ribs.

The chromatic waterfall formed as sound distorted. Instead of moving through it, everything froze. Time itself felt held, suspended in a crystal stillness that made Mari's skin prickle.

Mari Stonepaw, the Queen's voice entered her singular mind without invitation. *It would seem I've underestimated you and your friends.*

Greg's thought came sharp. *Mari, is everything okay? Why's the transit frozen?*

Jerro responded from the rear turret. *No—everything is not okay. We're being held back by a ship.*

It's not the ship holding us, Mari sent, frustration tightening her words.

The emblem on her forehead began to glow. Color drained from the chromatic fall as transit reversed, yanking them backward out of escape, the whole universe cinched tight by the throat.

Hang on. We're going home, Mari sent, blunt and final.

The triple diamond crest coursed with hot blue energy. She stepped away from the panel, and her body shuddered. A translucent silhouette of Mari remained at the controls, holding the ship steady.

Mari leaned down to Phlip, pressing her head to his, nose to nose, a moment that was too small for what it carried. Then she patted Squiggy's head, gentler than her urgency allowed. Squiggy's eyes widened, something in her going still, sensing a goodbye she didn't have language for.

Mari turned and sprinted out of the cockpit. All four limbs accelerated in coordination.

Her speed increased rapidly, leaving a blue energy streak behind her as she dove off the back of the ship, plummeting toward the smaller vessel holding them back. The enemy ship deployed cannons and sent a barrage into her, but the bolts deflected as a tight pod of energy formed around her body.

We burrow, Mari broadcasted calmly. The words carried more weight than instruction. They carried intention.

Mari impacted the ship, the Queens presence inside. It ruptured into halves, debris tumbling toward the planet's surface. A shockwave rippled outward, shifting from bright indigo into fiery yellow as it dissipated.

The projected Mari in the cockpit guided the controls as their ship lurched forward, riding the shockwave and slipping into the chromatic waterfall. Phlip and Squiggy watched as Mari's ephemeral visage pixelated into particulate, sweeping through them and then the ship as it passed into transit.

The ship roared back into open air, the last traces of color peeling away behind them, and into a place none of them recognized. The sky was a washed, bruised color, too pale to be comforting, with thin bands of cloud stretched like torn cloth. Below, the world was sand and stone. Dunes rolled away in uneven waves, the sand swirled through with lime-green particles that caught the light in sickly flashes. Rust-colored outcrops broke the slopes in jagged seams, rising like ribs from the ground. Heat shimmered off everything, and the light had a hard edge to it, as if it didn't belong here.

Sound snapped back and caught up all at once. Wind hammered the hull. Grit ticked against the glass.

Mari, Greg sent, pushing the thought outward with everything he had.

There was no answer. No flicker. Nothing at the edge.

His chest tightened. He tried again, sharper, then slower, changing the shape of the call, searching for any crack she could slip through. *Mari.* Still nothing. Only the thin pressure of his own mind meeting empty air.

Greg unbuckled and hurried through the hull, bursting into the cockpit. Phlip and Squiggy looked up at him as he entered, their faces too open for what had just happened.

"Where is she?" Greg shouted. The words fell into the wind and were gone.

Jerro arrived a half step behind him and climbed into the pilot's seat without speaking. His paws moved over the controls on instinct as he guided the ship down toward a low basin between two dune ridges, choosing a pocket where the wind broke and the rocks offered a thin kind of cover. He chose distance and didn't look at Greg. Space was the only thing he could offer.

The ship settled with a heavy hiss. Sand lifted and spun around them, then drifted down in a slow, relentless fall.

Greg stood frozen in the cockpit doorway, breathing too fast. His eyes kept scanning empty seats and narrow corridors. Maybe Mari had slipped past him. Maybe she was there somewhere. His throat worked once. No sound came out.

Phlip hopped close and pressed against Greg's leg, glassy eyes fixed on his face, searching for the missing piece there. Squiggy crept up behind Jerro and placed one small paw on his tail. Jerro flinched, then turned and saw her trembling, the effort it took to stay upright. He pulled her into a hug without thinking, holding on the way you hold on when something has already been taken.

Lunda was there too, quiet in the shared channel. She didn't speak. She didn't need to. She felt the hollow space Mari had left behind, and the grief that filled it.

CHAPTER 19 | RECURSION

Thick dust sealed Mari's eyelashes shut as cool, dank air enveloped her still form. She drew a ragged breath that caught, the dust heavy in her lungs. One arm swept out to trace the dirt-laden stone floor while the other paw rubbed her eyes free. A faint blue glow pooled in the cavern's corner, delicate and steady. She blinked into it, and her pupils widened.

She was back in the cave.

For a heartbeat, relief washed through her so hard it almost made her laugh.

A dream. It had been a dream.

Mari sat up too fast, and the world swam. The shattered mural spread across the wall in front of her, fractured exactly where it had been before. Familiar cracks. Familiar missing pieces. The same jagged lines cutting through imagery that had once been whole.

Relief curdled.

No. Not again.

Her mind reached back to the old solution. Let it blur. Let it drain out. Let the names slip away until there was nothing left but the cave and the quiet and the blank.

Pressure built behind her eyes instead, steady and rising, like her skull was filling with water.

She pressed a paw to her chest and forced a breath in. Then another. Slow. Measured. An anchor.

Stay.

The memories hit, but this time they didn't slide off her. They slammed in and held. The Burrow. Rufus. Station. Jerro and Greg. Phlip's warm weight when he leaned into her like he belonged there. Squiggy's small tremble that never stopped her from choosing to stay close. Prince Lukyaza. The Borruki. The Glorp. The Queen Regent's violet gaze.

All of it stacked together until she couldn't tell where one moment ended and another began.

My friends, she thought, and the thought tried to fray, tried to dissolve into the familiar blankness.

She clenched down on it.

"My friends," she said out loud, the words small and raw in the open air. Proof it wasn't a dream. Proof she was still here.

She swallowed hard and tried to breathe through the pressure rising in her throat. They had gone through the transit—she was sure of it. The certainty made her paws shake. She had held the connection by leaving a version of herself behind, astral and translucent, just long enough to get them home.

Home.

Where did home even land them? The question came with the next breath. She didn't know where they ended up, only that she had not gone with them. She could still feel the shape of that choice in her bones, like a burn that hadn't cooled yet.

She tried to reach Jerro and Greg, shoving her voice across the distance. *Nothing.* The channel was gone, cleanly cut.

Mari pushed herself to her feet, legs unsteady, and stumbled toward the passage she remembered crawling through the first time.

The rough stone scraped her fur as she squeezed through. She expected the rope to be there, dangling like it had before.

It was gone.

The absence hit her harder than it should have. That rope had been a window to her time. This was not then.

Mari closed her eyes and let her mind extend outward. She felt the space around her, not with sight but with that deeper sense she had learned to trust, the psionic architecture of the world brushing against her awareness. Her forehead throbbed with heat, followed by the pinging, metallic sensation that waited for her every time. She gathered what little remained, then lifted.

Weightless, she eased through the opening.

Darkness met her, soft and immense. A partial moon hung low in the sky, dim enough that shadows still owned most of the valley. Its light painted everything in a pale, quiet silver that did not feel welcoming, only present.

She drifted down and landed lightly on the ground, paws sinking into cool grass. The crisp floral air of Long Valley greeted her as she emerged from the hidden entrance. The boulder was still there, but it had split cleanly in two, a dark fracture running through its heart like something had finally given up. Grass had overtaken the tracks, erasing any trace of its past journey.

Mari stepped forward a few paces, then stopped as if her body remembered where to pause.

The night sky was clear and full of stars. She lay on her back, letting the grass cradle her, and stared upward into the vast emptiness those specks of light inhabited. Something cool between her eyes made her reflexively lift her paw. The symbol. It had gone cold, like a candle had been snuffed by ice.

For a moment she allowed herself to pretend she could hear Jerro's commentary about structures, Greg's impatience, Phlip's contented snorts, Lunda's quiet presence and Squiggy tucked somewhere close to the human.

The thought cracked, and loneliness slid into its place.

Mari blinked slowly. The stars above her seemed to sharpen, then soften, then shift. At first, she thought it was her vision, dust still clinging to her eyes, but the sky itself was moving. Not drifting like clouds. Rearranging.

The specks of light drew closer together in gentle arcs, pulling into lines that had not existed a moment before. A curve formed, then another. The outline of a muzzle. Eyes that weren't really eyes, but she recognized them anyway. A prominent nose. Incisors. Wisps of starlight stretched into the suggestion of old fur.

The face of the old marmot stared down at her from the sky.

It smiled.

Mari smiled back, the expression arriving before she could decide whether she wanted it. She felt tears sting her eyes, not from sadness alone, but from the weight of recognition, the sense that she had seen this before and would see it again.

How many times? She wondered, and the question did not feel like fear. It felt like the edge of a bigger truth.

The voice came then, not loud, not violent like the Queen's intrusion, but steady and intimate, like a thought placed gently into her mind.

The Burrowing Rodent Empire lives within you.

Mari exhaled into the night air, staring up at that starlit face as it held its shape, patient and knowing, with all the time in the universe.

And somewhere far away, in another light, her friends were without her.

Dillon Willett was born and raised in Las Vegas, Nevada, and now lives in Colorado with his wife and two children. He works as a civil engineer managing transportation infrastructure projects, but his off-hours belong to stories. Short-form content, worldbuilding, and an ever-evolving multiverse of burrowing rodent psionics grown alongside the Gopherit community.

A fan of sci-fi since childhood, Dillon has also spent decades playing Dungeons & Dragons and Dungeon Mastering campaigns— experience that shaped his love of character-driven adventure. *The Burrowing Rodent Empire: Origins* is his debut novel.

This is just the surface of what is to come. The multiverse is infinite, and so are his ideas.

See you in Sector 27

Alexandre Augusto, better known as Jiripoca when online, is a Brazilian natural and purveyor of all things creative.

From digital artwork, to writing and cosplay, Jiripoca has made it his mission to find and connect like-minded individuals with his creations and ideas and did not hesitate when invited to collaborate on *The Burrowing Rodent Empire: Origins.*

If you need me, bring snacks to the woods and whisper my name.

Instagram: @jiripoca_art

X: @jiripoca_xoxo

Bluesky: @jiripoca-art.bsky.social